Sunday Times best-selling author Vernon Coleman has sold over 2 million books in the UK alone. His books have been translated into 23 languages and sell in over 50 countries.

CAT FABLES

Vernon Coleman's book, *Cat Fables* begins with Korky, discovering he's not useless after all, in *The Cat Who Found Out He Was Special*. And Jack enjoys getting things off his chest in *The Good Listener*. Whilst in *Looking Down at Birds*, Robbie finds it more exhilarating to climb halfway up a tree than to watch someone climb to the top . . . Each tale has a moral, and is a joy for any cat lover.

Books by Vernon Coleman
Published by The House of Ulverscroft:

THE BILBURY CHRONICLES
BILBURY GRANGE
BILBURY REVELS
DEADLINE
BILBURY COUNTRY
IT'S NEVER TOO LATE
THE MAN WHO INHERITED
A GOLF COURSE
THE VILLAGE CRICKET TOUR
BILBURY PIE
AROUND THE WICKET
TOO MANY CLUBS AND
NOT ENOUGH BALLS
CAT TALES
BILBURY PUDDING

VERNON COLEMAN

◆

CAT FABLES

Complete and Unabridged

ULVERSCROFT
Leicester

First published in Great Britain in 2007 by
Chilton Designs
Devon

First Large Print Edition
published 2011
by arrangement with
Publishing House
Devon

British Library CIP Data

Coleman, Vernon.
  Cat fables.
  1. Cats- -Fiction.
  2. Fables.
  3. Large type books.
  I. Title
  823.9'14–dc22

  ISBN 978–1–44480–696–0

Published by
F. A. Thorpe (Publishing)
Anstey, Leicestershire

Set by Words & Graphics Ltd.
Anstey, Leicestershire
Printed and bound in Great Britain by
T. J. International Ltd., Padstow, Cornwall

This book is printed on acid-free paper

Dedication

If she had to choose another life she would, I know, come back not as a real life Princess, festooned with jewels and surrounded by servants, but as a cat; preferably, of course, a much-loved, over-indulged fluffy cat with a doting Upright. And so these stories about cats (which will, I hope, give her, and other cat lovers, an insight into the special world cats inhabit) are dedicated to my gentle love Donna Antoinette. All ways and always.

Contents

Definition

Cat (n) 'An animal which can, without any perceptible sense of embarrassment, continue to declare its innocence when all the evidence shows quite clearly and unequivocally that it is guilty.'

Vernon Coleman

Note

As readers of my eight other cat books will already know I use the word 'Upright' instead of the phrase 'human being'. The word was first used in this way by Alice in her two books *Alice's Diary* and *Alice's Adventures* and I have adopted this usage, in her memory, ever since.

Readers who are surprised to discover that cats talk to one another will find details of just how they do it in my book *The Secret Lives Of Cats* where I explain that cats communicate with one another by a form of telepathy known as 'felipathy'.

Foreword

We can learn a great deal from cats. I don't just mean that we can learn about their behaviour. We can also learn lessons that apply to us, too. Watch and listen to cats and we can learn an enormous amount that will help us through life.

How true are the stories in this book?

Well, that's for you to decide. I'm not telling. And nor are the cats.

But each story has been chosen because it contains a message; a 'moral' if you like.

So these aren't so much stories as fables or parables.

Vernon Coleman, Catland, 2007

The Cat who Found Out
He Was Special

Korky the cat lived in a large household. There were seven Uprights (two large ones, two medium sized ones and three small ones), three dogs (two large ones and a small one), two hamsters (both small), six white mice (also all small), six sheep (all large), a pig (large), a cow (huge), two horses (both huge), a snake (long and wriggly), eight chickens (medium sized) and a cat called Korky (cat sized).

Korky liked being a member of a large household.

But he was confused and unhappy.

His big problem was that when he looked around at all the creatures he lived with, he couldn't help feeling rather inadequate.

The dogs could bark and run much faster than he could.

The horses could carry the Uprights on their backs.

The cow could give milk.

The pig could make a wonderful sound and could eat just about anything without getting an upset tummy.

The white mice and the hamsters could hide in a small pile of wood shavings.

The sheep could produce wool with which the Uprights could make lovely jumpers.

The snake could kill its enemies with a single bite.

And the chickens could lay eggs.

Korky found all this quite daunting.

And the more he thought about things, the more depressed he became.

He didn't tell anyone about this for a long time.

'You seem preoccupied a lot these days,' said the small dog eventually.

Korky sighed and nodded.

'You've got something on your mind?'

Another nod from Korky. 'I look around and I feel so, well, so inadequate,' he said.

'Ah,' said the dog, who wasn't very good with problems of this type. (He was a very simple-minded dog who could bark and catch rats very well but who didn't put a lot of thought into more complex matters.) 'Have a word with the large, grey owl who lives in the hollow tree at the bottom of the field where the horses live,' said the dog. 'His consulting hours are 9 p.m. to 11 p.m. Mondays to Thursdays. You shouldn't have any trouble with his fee. He charges one mouse.'

'I doubt if he'll be able to help,' sighed Korky.

But he knew he didn't have anything to

lose and so when it got dark he trotted out of the house, picked up a mouse from behind the barn, and loped down the field to the hollow tree.

'I feel useless,' Korky told the owl, when he had handed over the mouse. 'Everyone else seems so special. In comparison, I feel decidedly ordinary.'

'Ordinary?' said the owl. 'What's ordinary?'

(The owl, being the wisest of all creatures, knew very well what 'ordinary' meant. But he was so wise that he knew that if he was going to be able to help he needed to know what Korky meant by it.)

'Ordinary means not very special,' replied Korky. 'All these other creatures can do things that I can't do.'

'And you think that makes them special?'

Korky nodded.

'What can you do that they can't do?'

Korky shook his head. 'Nothing,' he said, sadly.

'You're wrong,' said the wise owl. He flapped his wing and uttered a leisurely too wit too woo. He liked to keep in practice. 'What do you like doing best of all?'

Korky thought for a moment. 'I like sleeping in the airing cupboard,' he said at last. 'I sleep on the top shelf. I've worked out a way to wriggle up from the lower shelves.'

'Can the pig do that?' asked the wise owl.

3

'Oh no,' said Korky, with a smile.
'The cow?'
'Definitely not.'
'The horse?'
Korky shook his head.

'Can you do anything else?' asked the wise
owl. 'What do you do with the Uprights?'
    'There's a tiny Upright in a Skirt,' said Korky.
'I make her happy. I sit on her lap and let her
stroke my fur. That always makes her feel good.'

'Can the snake do that?'

'Definitely not,' said Korky.

'Can the chickens do that?'

'No,' said Korky.

'So why do you say that the others can do things that you can't do?' said the wise owl. He gazed into the distance for a moment and produced another too wit too woo.

'I hadn't thought of it like that,' said Korky, who couldn't understand why he felt much happier than he'd felt for a long, long time.

'What you have to remember is that you're just as special in your way as the others are in their special ways,' said the wise owl. 'Now go away while I eat this nice mouse you brought me. And stop feeling so sorry for yourself.'

'Yes,' said Korky, his fears and inadequacies banished. 'Thank you very much Mr Owl.'

And, full of pride for the first time in his life, he skipped and danced all the way back home.

Moral

A cow drinks water and makes milk. A snake drinks water and makes poison. A cat drinks cream and goes to sleep in the airing cupboard.

The Man Who Hated Cats

Two cats called Ginger and Tiger lived with a family of Uprights who really loved animals.

The Uprights had a large, old-fashioned terraced house in the middle of a big city. There were four Uprights: Mr Jellicoe, Mrs Jellicoe, Lucinda Jellicoe (aged 8) and Roger Jellicoe (aged 6). And apart from Ginger and Tiger the household consisted of two Labrador dogs (Henry and Gilbert), five white mice (Mickey, Dicky, Tricky, Picky and Nicky who were supposed to live in a large cage in Roger's bedroom but who spent most of their time out of it and only went back through the tiny door when Ginger and Tiger were spotted in the vicinity) and a large goldfish called Oswald who lived in a tank.

By and large all these creatures (including the Uprights but with the possible exception of Oswald) lived together very happily and confrontations were as rare as snow at Christmas.

The house was large enough for everyone (except Oswald) to be able to do their own thing. The garden was large and mature and included trees for climbing, bushes for hiding

6

in and a large lawn suitable for racing around on if the weather wasn't too hot and you were that way inclined.

There was, of course, a snag.

The snag was the neighbour on the left hand side (looking towards the bottom of the garden).

The neighbour was a man called Mr Loosemore who hated all animals but who hated cats most of all.

Mr Loosemore hated cats so much that he did everything he possibly could to prevent them from entering his garden at all. He had put barbed wire along the whole length of the fence which separated his garden from the Jellicoes' garden. He had chopped down most of the trees which had once proved such an innocent attraction to neighbourhood cats and he had concreted over a patch of shrubbery which had once been a favourite haunt of those cats who liked hunting mice, voles, shrews and other small creatures.

And, just to make his views about cats as clear as clear could be, he used to spend several hours a day sitting in wait — just in case a cat ever dared to enter his garden. He would sit on his terrace armed with two buckets of water and an air rifle. Any cat who dared to enter his garden did so knowing that if he was spotted the consequences would be dire.

Naturally, although they had a large garden of their own (and it has to be said that as far as cats were concerned they were very fortunate creatures) Ginger and Tiger were constantly attracted to the forbidden garden which lay on the other side of the barbed wire topped fence.

'There is,' said Ginger, 'something irresistible

about anything which is forbidden.'

Eventually, of course, the irresistibility of venturing into next door's garden gradually overcame all their well-founded fears.

And when Ginger found a small gap at the bottom of the fence there was no longer any chance that they could resist their natural inclination to disobey.

They thought about going through the gap late at night, when Mr Loosemore was in bed and his garden lay unguarded and in darkness. 'But, where's the fun in that?' asked Ginger. 'There's no point in breaking the rules if no one knows you're breaking them.'

So, they went through the fence at four o'clock in the afternoon when Mr Loosemore was sitting on his terrace, alert and watchful and, above all, armed.

He saw them, of course.

They would, if they'd been honest, have admitted that they would have been disappointed if he hadn't.

He saw them as they raced up the tallest of his remaining two horse chestnut trees and he lost them as they disappeared among the leaves of the upper branches.

He was too far away to use his buckets of water and so he fired his air rifle at them. Unable to see his two targets he fired into the leaves where he thought the two cats might be. He loaded his gun as quickly as he could, with fingers fumbling with impotent rage.

Ginger and Tiger stayed up the tree for an hour until it started to get dark. Then, as stealthily as they could manage, they crept down the far side of the tree and darted back to the hole in the fence and to safety.

'Phew,' sighed Ginger, when they got back home. He shook a leaf out of his fur. 'That was exciting.' He had to make a big effort to stop his voice shaking. He didn't want Tiger to know how frightened he had been.

'I'm glad we did that!' said Tiger, trying to stop his voice shaking so that Ginger would not know how frightened he had been.

'We certainly showed him,' said Ginger.

'It's not as nice as our garden though,' said Tiger.

'No,' agreed Ginger immediately. 'It's definitely not as nice as our garden.'

'No real need to go back there,' said Tiger.

'No,' said Ginger. 'No point at all.'

Moral
***If you obey all the rules you'll miss
rather a lot of fun. So, ignore
the rules occasionally. If you don't
ignore the rules at least some of
the time there is no point in there
being any rules.***

The Cat Magician

Wobbly had lived with the Gritsby family for four years. In fact, she couldn't really remember ever not living with the Gritsbys. It was the only life she knew.

She had arrived at the Gritsbys' home via Sharon Gritsby, the younger of two daughters, who had acquired her from a schoolfriend. And her arrival had not been welcomed universally.

'What the devil have you brought that creature here for?' demanded Mr Gritsby, a stern, bully of a man who had some deep permanent frown lines etched onto his face and who regarded laughter as something frivolous

people did when they didn't have enough work to keep them busy.

'Don't expect me to clean up after it,' snapped Mrs Gritsby, a huge, billowy woman who spent most of her time sitting around the house eating biscuits and chocolates and complaining about the mess by which she was constantly surrounded.

'Yuk,' it's so plain looking, said Tracey, Sharon's older sister. 'If you have to have a kitten couldn't you have found a pretty one?'

You will not be surprised to hear that none of this made Wobbly feel welcome. (And, indeed, the name she was given — Wobbly — while undoubtedly accurate at the time, did nothing to improve the nervous kitten's fragile self-confidence.)

During the weeks and months which followed Wobbly found that life with the Gritsby family was, to say the least, difficult and, to say the most, nigh on unbearable. The cool welcome she had received on her arrival did not warm with time. Indeed, on the contrary, things got steadily worse.

Sharon got tired of her new fluffy toy — especially when she realised that it needed to be fed twice a day. Tracey complained constantly that the kitten had chewed her slippers or had left hairs on the clothes she scattered on the floor of her bedroom. And Mr and

Mrs Gritsby just complained a lot, invariably managing to blame Wobbly for everything that happened that they didn't like.

By the end of her first year in the Gritsby household Wobbly was, if anything, even more nervous and wobbly than she had been when she'd arrived.

The months passed by, and, as they have a recurring tendency to do, the years went with them, and with every passing season Wobbly lost more confidence and became ever more nervous, ever more fearful and ever more apprehensive. When one of the Gritsby daughters spoke to her she would shiver and shrink a little. When one of the grown up Gritsbys spoke her heart would thump so much she thought it would burst.

By the end of the fourth year Wobbly had become a nervous cat; eyes constantly darting here and there, muscles always twitching; always just a whisker away from panic. If anyone bent down to touch her she would shiver and shake and then run away and hide. She did not know the joy of spending an evening on a warm lap. But she knew only too well the pain of spending a night cowering under a car in a neighbour's driveway because there was nowhere else to go to hide from the rain on a dark and stormy night.

And then Miss Pilbeam moved into the

bungalow five doors down the road. Sweet, gentle, delicate, fragile Miss Pilbeam. A septuagenarian. A little frail, with arthritis in her hips and knees, but alert and lively nevertheless. A former school teacher. Loved by generations of mixed infants. Alone in the world now because her much-loved long-standing feline companion Marmalade had died just five months earlier.

They met just a week away from the fourth anniversary of Wobbly's unhappy meeting with the Gritsbys. It was dark. It was raining. And Wobbly, booted out of the house by a particularly bad-tempered Mr Gritsby, had been hiding under Miss Pilbeam's elderly Morris Minor. (The model with the soft top. She'd bought it when new and if ever sold the garage would tell no lie if they advertised it as having had 'one careful lady owner'.)

Miss Pilbeam had gone to the door to put her empty milk bottles on the step and even in the dark she saw the fearful and trembling Wobbly cowering next to the left rear wheel. She was well able to recognise a cat in need when she saw one.

Her attempts to persuade the cat to come to her failed miserably at first.

But Miss Pilbeam was an experienced cat magician. She knew that the most direct route to a cat's heart is via its stomach and a tin of best salmon emptied out and crushed on a bone china saucer was all it took. Wobbly hadn't eaten for three days. Not unless you count the congealed corpse of a two day dead spider and a few crumbs of broken biscuit which she'd dragged out from underneath a chair in the living room.

And then Miss Pilbeam filled a saucer with condensed milk.

And followed that with a cereal bowl containing fresh, cold custard from a tin.

All delivered while Wobbly remained cowering underneath Miss Pilbeam's elderly vehicle.

'Oh you poor starving creature,' said the kindly Miss Pilbeam, reaching out to stroke Wobbly's head.

Wobbly backed away instinctively. Kindness was something to which she was not yet quite accustomed and her instincts had kept her alive. When one of the Gritsbys reached out it was usually to hit her or to pick her up and throw her off a chair or bed.

'Why don't you come in and lie by the fire?' invited Miss Pilbeam. 'I won't hurt you.' She waved a hand behind her, in the direction of the front door which she had left open.

Still, Wobbly remained where she was; too frightened to make a move. What if Miss Pilbeam turned out to be a felicidal maniac? What if Miss Pilbeam, harmless and kindly as she appeared to be, turned out to be catching cats for a vivisector? Wobbly was consumed with fears and anxieties. The Gritsby household wasn't exactly welcoming, and love and food were in pretty short supply there, but at least none of the Gritsbys had actually tried to kill her. Not deliberately anyway.

'What's your name?' asked Miss Pilbeam. She reached forward very slowly and checked the fur around Wobbly's neck. 'You haven't got an identity tag,' she said disapprovingly.

Wobbly, who had been brought up in a house where Uprights screeched and shouted, liked Miss Pilbeam's soft and soothing voice. She edged forward an inch or two. The cold custard had really been very pleasant. She'd never eaten so well before. Miss Pilbeam seemed gentle and reassuring.

'There's nothing to worry about,' said Miss Pilbeam, reassuringly. She paused and thought for a moment. When she thought she held her head slightly to one side, rather like a bird. 'I think I'll call you Rosie,' she said finally. Wobbly pricked up her ears. She liked the name Rosie. She thought it sounded rather fine. She liked it much better than Wobbly. She had never liked *that* name. She edged forwards a little more. But she was still prepared to turn and run if necessary. She was still very nervous; still anxious about what might happen.

But Miss Pilbeam resisted the temptation to make any quick movements. She knew just how nervous cats could be. 'I can see that you're frightened,' she said to Rosie. 'But I tell you what I'll do. I'll go in now because I'm getting rather cold. But I'll leave the front door open. If you want to come in and sit by my fireside you'll be very, very welcome.' And with that Miss Pilbeam turned away and went back into her little bungalow. At the doorway she turned back for an instant. She bent down so that she could see underneath the car and then she smiled. 'Do come in,' she said, with an encouraging smile. 'It's so cold

and miserable out here but indoors it's toasty warm and we can keep each other company.'

It was another three minutes before Rosie, formerly Wobbly, finally found the courage to enter Miss Pilbeam's house. She stood on the step for a moment, her ears pricked, every muscle tensed, every nerve taut. She wanted to turn and run. But she couldn't. She had to know. She had to know if Miss Pilbeam was as good as she seemed to be. And so Rosie moved forwards a few inches. And waited again. And then moved forward another few inches.

Finally, summoning up all her courage, Rosie suddenly bounded forward towards the light in Miss Pilbeam's living room. Once inside the room she stopped suddenly and looked around. There was a blazing log fire in the hearth. Miss Pilbeam, sitting in a comfortable old chair on one side of the fire, smiled at her.

'Hello, Rosie,' she said. 'I'm glad you came.' She bent down and stroked Rosie's head and back. She lowered her voice to a whisper. 'You and I are going to be the very best of friends,' she said. 'I'll just go and shut the front door and lock out all that nasty weather and then we'll settle down together, you and I, and have a nice chat by the fire.'

And that's how Wobbly became Rosie and

how Rosie found a new home and a new very best friend.

Moral

If you don't take chances, you'll never know what might have happened. And you'll always wonder. And always regret.

The Fishing Expedition

Tabatha was the most kind-hearted cat anyone had ever met. Everyone agreed on this.

With Uprights she was unfailingly patient and appreciative. She loved being stroked and tickled under the chin and even when a hand rubbed her fur the wrong way she remained calm and content. With the slightest encouragement she would roll over onto her back and allow her tummy to be tickled. She was wonderful with children; never scratching or hissing and always taking part in the roughest of their games without so much as a momentary protest.

She was similarly patient with other cats.

The Uprights with whom she lived had, over the years, acquired three other cats in addition to Tabatha. There was Micky (a boisterous black and white who loved climbing on shelves), Honey (a delicate and rather highly strung short-haired Persian whose greatest joy in life was sitting in the sun) and Poppy (a six month old kitten who just liked playing).

Although Tabatha was the oldest, and most

senior of these cats, she did not behave like a Prima Donna (as so many cats do when they are the senior member of a household) and she did not expect the others to adapt their lives to suit hers. Many cats who suddenly find themselves sharing a home with another animal will behave boorishly and expect their habits and preferences to be respected. Tabatha wasn't like that. If she found another cat sleeping in one of her favourite spots she would simply move on and sleep somewhere else. If Poppy wanted to play then Tabatha would play — even if she would rather have had a snooze.

But, not surprisingly, Tabatha's kindness, patience, understanding and willingness to please (allied to an unwillingness to dis-please) meant that she often ended up doing things that she really didn't want to do and didn't enjoy doing.

In addition to Micky, Honey and Poppy there were a number of other cats living in the immediate neighbourhood and among all of these it was widely known that Tabatha was always ready to please; forever willing to do things she didn't really want to do if it would make another cat happy.

So, when Hector, who lived two houses away, came round and told Tabatha that he wanted her to join him on a fishing expedition he did so not caring whether or not she wanted to go fishing, but knowing that she would agree.

It wasn't just any fishing expedition.

Hector had for some time, had his eye on the fish who lived in a pond in a nearby garden.

But there was, of course, a snag for this was no ordinary pond, these were no ordinary fish and catching them was no ordinary fishing expedition.

The pond owner, an elderly retired army Colonel told everyone he had a war wound but he actually had bad arthritis. He walked with the aid of a large blackthorn stick. Apart from his military experiences (something he was always happy to talk about) the Colonel was very proud of his fish (a mixture of gold-fish and koi carp) which he regarded as the best in the neighbourhood.

The Colonel (as he insisted on being called) had lost several fish to a visiting heron and two to cats. His attempts to scare away these poachers had proved fruitless because his gammy leg meant that he could not match his threats with physical action and so he had, in response, set up a simple but effective defence system to prevent any further losses.

The defence system the Colonel had devised involved purchasing a large Rott-weiler which he kept hungry and which he allowed to roam free in the garden.

'The danger,' explained Hector, 'is that if I'm catching a fish the dog might come up behind me. So your job will be to act as lookout while I catch a fish.'

'What do I do if I see the dog?' asked Tabatha. 'Should I make a noise so that you'll know it's time to run?'

'No, no,' said Hector. 'Your job is to run around the garden with the dog chasing you so that I can get away with the fish.'

'But that's dangerous!' said Tabatha.

'No, no, not at all,' said Hector, with all the confidence and assurance of a cat who would not be exposed to any danger whatsoever. 'You just allow the dog to get close enough to you to think he's going to catch you — so that he doesn't worry about me — while staying far enough ahead of him to make sure that he doesn't actually get close enough to catch you.'

Tabatha didn't like the sound of this at all and looked very doubtful.

'Don't look like that,' said Hector, cheerily. 'I'm relying on you. I can't do this without you.'

Tabatha blinked but didn't say anything. There was a lot she could have said. She could have pointed out that Hector had rarely ever even bothered to speak to her before.

She could have pointed out that Hector had lots of much closer chums who could have helped him. She could have explained that her Uprights gave her cooked fish every Friday and Tuesday (nicely filleted and served in a creamy sauce) and so she didn't need to risk her life helping Hector catch a fresh one. She could have simply said 'No' and walked away.

But she didn't say any of this.

Tabatha didn't like to say 'No' and so she said 'Yes'.

The fishing trip was a disaster.

After chasing Tabatha up a tree the Rottweiler turned his attention to Hector and chased him into the middle of the pond where, dripping wet and with a flower on his head, Hector escaped a nasty death by sitting on top of a small fountain. (His only stroke of good fortune was that the fountain was turned off at the time.)

It was eleven o'clock that night when the Rottweiler, called by the Colonel for his late supper, went into the house. And it was ten past eleven before Tabatha arrived home. She was dirty, tired, frightened and hungry and had absolutely nothing to show for a horrible day.

'If only I'd said 'No',' said Tabatha to herself, as she dragged herself through the cat flap and into the house. 'If I'd said 'No' I would, by now, be warm, fed and dreaming of rabbits.'

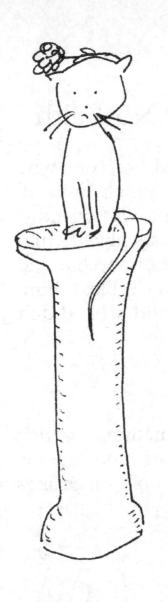

Hector escaped a
nasty death by
sitting in top of a
small fountain.

Moral

**When you have difficulty saying 'No'
to something you don't want to do
just remember how much more difficult things will be if you say 'Yes'.**

The Cat Who Had No Faith

Dick was a very pretty cat and everyone who knew him liked him very much indeed. Uprights liked him because he was friendly, patient and loyal. Other cats liked him because he was trustworthy, honourable and generous. Even dogs and mice liked him. There was no one in the world who didn't think Dick was wonderful.

Except.

There was one exception.

And that was Dick himself.

Dick suffered from something which psychiatrists and psychologists and people who read the posher sort of magazines usually call 'low self-esteem'.

By which it is meant that he had absolutely no faith in himself.

He regarded himself as someone to whom bad things always happened.

He expected bad things to happen. And he thought he deserved

to have bad things happen to him.

Inevitably, of course, when you expect bad things to happen they usually do.

Dick's great ambition had always been to be able to jump up onto the flat roof of the small extension at the back of the house where he lived.

This may seem to be a strange ambition but there was a good reason for it.

When he had been a kitten, and had first moved in with the Uprights called the Wainwrights, there had been an older cat called Tom living there. And as a young kitten Dick had once watched, with absolute astonishment and awe, as Tom had leapt from the terrace up onto the flat roof, where he had lain down and sunbathed in cat-perfect peace and quiet for the whole afternoon. Tom hadn't made it in one jump of course. There had been a good deal of scratching and clawing involved. He had used a piece of trellis, a clothes prop which always leant against the side of the shed and some thick strands of ivy which covered the lower two thirds of the wall. But it had, nevertheless, been a mighty impressive climb.

After Tom's death, Dick had tried to get up onto the flat roof on at least two dozen occasions. He had scrabbled and scrambled and clung and pulled at every available

27

pawhold and clawhold. He had broken several claws in the attempts. But he had always failed as, in his heart, he always knew he would. A foot or two from the flat roof he would feel all his strength leave him. He would be filled with hopelessness. And he would fall back to the ground with a painful thump.

Dick decided that Tom had been a very special cat. A supercat among mortals. A hero. A giant among cats. And he decided that the leap was impossible.

Then, one day, Dick lay on the grass watching a blackbird trying to break open a snail's shell. Time and time again the blackbird hammered the snail against a rock in the garden rockery. Several times the blackbird flew up into the air with the snail and then dropped it onto the patio paving. The blackbird kept trying for far longer than Dick had thought it possible for any creature to try to do anything. The bird just wouldn't give up. It persevered as though its life depended upon what it was doing. It devoted every bit of its concentration and energy to the task. It took no notice of Dick even though he was lying no more than thirty feet away. And in the end the snail's shell smashed. And the blackbird got its reward.

It was just the stimulus Dick needed.

I can do it, he said to himself.

If I try really hard and put every ounce of effort into getting up onto that roof I can get there. Once I'm nearly there I just have to keep going. I just need to have faith in myself.

And so he had faith.

He took a big breath. He tensed all his muscles. He looked up at the flat roof and, in his mind, saw himself sitting there.

He backed away from the wall a few feet. And then he ran, he leapt, he pulled, he scrabbled, he clawed, he stretched and he used every ounce of power and every bit of determination he could find.

And suddenly he was up there on the flat roof. Looking round. Breathless with exertion and excitement. Amazed and proud. It felt oh so good to be on top; to have achieved what had seemed for so long to be the impossible.

'Oh there you are, Dick!' said a familiar voice.

Dick looked down.

Mrs Wainwright was holding a brand new kitten. 'This is our new kitten,' she said, holding up the kitten so that Dick could get a better look. 'We're calling him Harry,' she said.

'Hello,' said Dick. He tried to look blasé, though no one but a kitten would have been fooled.

'That's Dick up there.' Mrs Wainwright told the kitten.

The kitten looked up at Dick.

And even Dick could see the awe and admiration in the kitten's eyes.

The kitten was looking up at him, he knew, in exactly the same way that he had once looked up at Tom.

Dick felt wonderful. He purred down at the kitten and nodded a welcome greeting.

Moral

**If you think you're going to fail then you will almost certainly fail.
If you think you will succeed
. . . well, at least you'll have a chance.**

A Cat With Two Tails

Coffee had always loved her tail. She loved to chase it ('It's much better than mice,' she told her friend Kipper. 'It's always there when you want it and, in the end, we both know that I'll always catch it.') And when she went to sleep she loved to wrap her tail over her nose. It was, she told Kipper, a toy, a muff and a good companion.

Coffee was six-years-old when it first occurred to her that if one tail was good, two tails should be twice as good.

'Why on earth would you want two tails?' Kipper asked her.

'I could keep my nose twice as warm,' replied Coffee. 'And I would have twice as much fun chasing two tails as I have chasing one.'

All Coffee's friends tried to convince her that having an extra tail would add nothing to the quality of her life. Some even attempted to convince her that an extra tail would be a burden not a boon.

'An extra tail would get in the way,' said one.

'Dogs would laugh at you,' said another.

But Coffee would not be shaken from her belief that two tails would be twice as much fun as one.

She had nursed this unusual longing for two years when her friend Kipper met her one morning with some startling news.

'I've just heard about a cat in Oaksville who has two tails!' announced Kipper excitedly. 'They were talking about it on the television last night.'

'A cat with two tails?' said Coffee. 'I have to see it.'

'We'll go tomorrow,' said Kipper. 'If we set off early in the morning we ought to be able to get there and back in a day. I'll be outside your back door at sunrise.'

Coffee didn't sleep a wink that night. She was sitting on the back door step waiting for Kipper to arrive long before the sun had poked its uppermost tip over the horizon.

And it was still dark when they set off.

'I knew you wouldn't be able to sleep,' said Kipper, who was that rarest of all God's creatures: 'a good friend'. 'So I came early.'

They travelled for hours and Coffee never stopped talking about the cat with two tails. 'How did it come about?' she wanted to know.

'I think it runs in the family,' explained

Kipper. 'His mother's brother had two tails too.'

'Oh, how I'd love to be a member of that family,' said Coffee.

It was three in the afternoon when the two cats, tired and paw weary, finally arrived at their destination.

'I'll wait here for you,' said Kipper, sitting down at the gate leading to the house where the cat with two tails lived.

And so Coffee went on alone. And met the famous cat with two tails.

It was quite a disappointment for Coffee.

The cat with two tails was very bad tempered and not at all pleased to receive yet another visitor.

'But isn't it wonderful to have two tails?' asked Coffee.

'No,' snapped the cat with two tails, quite sharply. 'If I try to chase my tail I get confused and dizzy. That's no fun at all.'

'But isn't it good to be able to wrap two tails around your nose when the weather is cold?' asked Coffee.

'No,' came the firm reply. 'It gets far too hot.'

And so Coffee turned away and went back up the path to where Kipper was waiting.

'How did it go? Do you still wish you had two tails? asked Kipper.

'Let's go home,' said Coffee.

And from that day on she was very happy with the one tail she'd got. Never again did she wish she had two.

Moral

Twice as much of something isn't necessarily twice as good.

The Green Green Grass
Of Home

Daisy and Maisy were twins. They looked exactly alike. They were both two thirds black and one third white. They had identical white smudges under their chins. They walked in precisely the same way. They sounded just the same — whether they were purring or miaowing. They both had a habit of jumping up into the air and turning round if they were startled from behind. They both had one ear which drooped over a little at the tip.

For most of their short lives the two cats lived in an apartment in a converted house in a busy part of the city. They lived there with their Uprights (a nice young couple who both worked in something called corporate affairs). It was a pleasant, sunny apartment, though not very big, and since they knew no different, and had never in their lives been out of doors, Maisy and Daisy were very happy there.

But then the Uprights, together with Daisy and Maisy, moved to a house in the suburbs.

And after a long journey in two separate wicker carrying cages (which neither cat liked very much but which they didn't find too intolerable because their cages were kept side by side in the car and they could see one another through gaps in the wickerwork and, best of all, they could talk to and therefore reassure one another) Daisy and Maisy suddenly found themselves exploring a brand new house.

There was a downstairs and an upstairs.

And connecting the two there were stairs!

What a delight stairs proved to be.

The two cats raced up them. And they sat at the top and looked down. And then they raced down them. And then they raced up and down and up and down and up and down until they were exhausted and they lay on the new carpet and closed their eyes and had a catnap.

They liked the stairs.

And then, oh then, the twins discovered the garden.

The Upright in a Skirt opened a door and the Upright in Trousers walked out into a huge open space and called to them.

'It's OK,' he said. 'Come on.'

Daisy looked at Maisy.

And Maisy looked at Daisy.

For a moment neither of them moved.

'It's all right,' said the Upright in a Skirt. 'You'll enjoy it. We moved here so that you'd have a garden to explore. It's all yours!'

Daisy took a sniff. The air out here smelt different. Fresher. Cooler. Altogether different. She sniffed again. There were a dozen new smells. No, more than a dozen. A hundred. Smells she'd never come across before. She turned to Maisy and sniffed, showing her sister that she should sniff too.

So Maisy sniffed. And she, in turn, found herself entranced by all the new smells.

Encouraged by their Uprights, the two cats stepped a little further outside and began to explore. To begin with they stayed close together, but as they grew in confidence so they moved a little away from one another.

Eventually, they discovered a huge green

expanse. A soft, neatly trimmed green lawn. Softer than the softest carpet. Bigger than the biggest carpet they'd ever seen. And full of far more exciting smells than any carpet they'd ever known. There were even creatures living in it!

They spent the rest of the day racing around on the lawn. They ran on it. They walked on it. They sat on it. They rolled on it. This, they agreed, was even better than the stairs.

'It's your lawn,' said the Uprights. 'Yours to enjoy.'

Maisy and Daisy were in heaven.

On the second day in their new home Maisy and Daisy discovered the tree at the bottom of the lawn. And they found that if they used their claws they could climb up it. From the fork in the tree, where the main trunk divided into its main branches, the two cats could see over the fence.

And on the other side of the fence they saw another lawn.

The difference was that this one was much, much greener than the one in their own garden.

'If it looks that green how soft must it be?' asked Maisy.

'It must smell even better than our own lawn,' said Daisy, though to be honest she couldn't imagine how anything could smell better than their own lawn.

And so the two cats decided that they had to climb over the fence and take a look.

They went over the fence that afternoon.

And rushed onto the oh so very green lawn.

'Ouch!' said Daisy.

'It's nasty!' said Maisy.

'It's spiky and rough,' said Daisy.

'It hurts my paws when I walk on it,' said Maisy.

'And it smells absolutely horrid,' said Daisy.

'I don't care what it looks like, I don't like it,' said Maisy.

'Nor me,' agreed Daisy.

And so the two cats went home and played on their own lawn. It wasn't quite so green as the artificial grass the neighbour had lain down. But it was much softer and it smelt much better.

Moral

**The grass may look greener on the other side.
But looks aren't everything.**

Calendar Girl

Once upon a time, not very long ago, there were five cats. They were called Betty, Toby, Jeremy, Sadie and Scoobie and they all lived in identical houses in a very pleasant lane on the outskirts of a lovely, quiet little town in the heart of the very greenest stretch of gently rolling English countryside.

For several years the five cats were the very best of chums. They did everything together. One for all and all for one. They met one another every day (and sometimes, when they could all get out, every night too) and they did all the things normal, healthy cats do when they get together. They compared notes about their Uprights and shared mild moans when they had been offered inferior food. They amused one another with stories of how much fun they had had trying to teach their Uprights how to hunt. (On quiet days Jeremy would tell how his Upright, who never made any attempt to hunt, would respond to the appearance of a mouse by clambering onto the nearest chair and shouting 'Help!' until Sadie's Upright, who lived next door, and whose hunting skills, though described by

40

Sadie only as barely adequate, were unanimously agreed to be the best in the lane, came round and rescued her). And, when they were out together sitting in a huddle on wintry nights, when slivers of moonbeam turned innocent but gnarled and twisted tree branches into shadowy, snarling Rottweilers, scared one another with stories of ghosts and cat-chasing ghouls and did so so effectively that their hair all stood on end. Those were the times they loved most of all because cats, like children, love being scared when they know in their hearts that nothing terrible is going to happen to them.

They were the best of pals and it was the best of times.

And then the calendar happened.

It was, as these things usually are, unforeseen and unforeseeable.

We all of us, Uprights and cats alike, worry about the bad things which might happen to us but in the end the bad things that really do happen, and which take away our appetite in the daytime and our sleep at night, are the things we never worry about in advance because we never see them coming.

No one worried about the calendar because no one had any idea there was even going to be a calendar.

It started, as these things often do, with the

very best of intentions. And it started because Scoobie's Upright in Trousers had a sister who was married to a photographer and the sister and her photographer husband, who lived in the far north of the country, stopped off for the night at Scoobie's house because they were going to France for their summer holiday and needed somewhere to stay and rest before they drove down to Dover to catch the ferry across the English Channel.

And the photographer had, four days before coming away, been given a commission to deliver twelve original, engaging and amusing photographs of playful cats with which a publisher could create a calendar to be sold to those Uprights who are so besotted with cats that, when they are checking on the date of their next dental appointment, or sneaking a look to see what day of the week their birthday will be on, prefer to flick through pictures of cats rather than pictures of snow-clad mountain tops or rose-covered thatched cottages.

The photographer had forgotten that his wife's relatives had a cat but when he entered the spare bedroom and saw Scoobie sprawled in a patch of sunlight he was so taken with the image which was, he knew, just what he wanted for a page on his commissioned calendar, that he hurried back to the car, grabbed his camera, rushed back upstairs and took half a dozen pictures of his feline niece without Scoobie having any idea what was going on.

And that was it.

Scoobie never even knew that she was having her photograph taken. She didn't pose. She wasn't brushed or combed so that she would look her best. She was just lying, eyes shut, enjoying a patch of warmth on the window seat in the spare bedroom.

Having taken his pictures the photographer put down his camera and went downstairs to have a nice cup of tea and two slices of home-made ginger cake.

It wasn't until six months later that anyone knew that Scoobie was pictured on a calendar.

When the large, flat cardboard packet was delivered to the door one December morning neither of Scoobie's Uprights had any idea what it contained. And it wasn't until they read the note that accompanied the calendar, and turned to July, that they realised that Scoobie was famous.

That was when Scoobie's Uprights made their mistake.

Instead of simply putting the calendar on one side, ready to replace the soon to be expired (and, it has to be said, exceedingly dull) calendar containing twelve views of the Australian outback, currently hanging on the kitchen wall, they rushed upstairs to where Scoobie was having her after breakfast nap.

And they showed her the calendar.

They showed her the picture of herself.

At first Scoobie didn't take much notice. It was, she saw immediately, a photograph of herself asleep on the window seat in the spare bedroom. Naturally, since she had been asleep at the time, she had no recollection of the photograph ever being taken. It did not seem anything special.

It was Scoobie's Uprights who did the damage.

'Look,' said her Upright in Trousers, flicking through the pages of the calendar to show her the other photographs. 'You're Miss July!'

'You're a star!' said Scoobie's Upright who wears a Skirt, compounding the error.

Scoobie lifted up her head, examined the photograph more closely and began to purr with pride. She was a star. She was a calendar cat. She would no longer consider herself to be, or allow herself to be treated as, a normal cat. She was special. 'Of course, I always knew I was special,' she told the other cats on many subsequent occasions.

She told them this when they wanted her to

44

go mousing in the field at the bottom of Betty's garden.

'I have to be careful,' Scoobie explained. 'I might get my fur muddy if I go into the field. It's a long way from home and if it rains I'll get bedraggled. I wouldn't want my fans to see me looking a mess.'

None of the other cats wanted to upset her so none of them pointed out that as far as they knew she didn't have any fans and that, as far as they all knew, the only people who had seen the calendar were her own Uprights.

She reminded her friends that she was special when they wanted her to climb trees, chase butterflies in Mr Tavistock's cabbage patch or stay up all night being scared half to death by imaginary Rottweilers on the lawn behind the house where Toby lived.

And because she considered herself special she stopped doing the things she'd enjoyed so much before she'd become special.

She stopped hanging around outside the fishmonger's shop, waiting for the fishmonger's boy to put out the bin full of unwanted fish heads. She said it wasn't the sort of thing a cat like her ought to be seen doing.

She started staying indoors more and more often. She lay on the window seat where she had been photographed by her Upright's sister's husband, trying to recreate the pose which had made her special. She spent hours sitting in the kitchen staring up at the calendar and wondering how long it would be before July came and her picture took pride of place.

Scoobie's Upright in Trousers used to tear the pages off the calendar as the months went by. He would screw up the literally out-of-date pages and toss them into the kitchen rubbish bin along with discarded tea bags, broken egg shells and the bedraggled looking cabbage leaves that no one, not even the caterpillars, ever eat.

Scoobie looked forward to July but at the same time she half dreaded it. What would happen at the end of her month? What would her Upright in Trousers do with her photograph? Every day of the month she stared up at herself and wondered. Having her photograph on a calendar no longer seemed quite such a good thing. Now that she thought of herself as being special she was frightened that she would stop being special. What had been a source of such pride quickly became a source of great anxiety. Suddenly being Miss July didn't seem quite as important as it had seemed before.

And suddenly Scoobie knew that there was

something she had to do. She knew what it was that was really important in her life.

She went outside and set off in search of Betty, Sadie, Toby and Jeremy.

It was raining slightly and it didn't take long to find them. They were sheltering on the porch of the summerhouse in Toby's garden.

'If you're doing anything exciting today would you mind if I joined in?' Scoobie asked, rather tentatively.

'Of course not,' said Toby immediately. He paused. 'But are you sure you don't mind? You won't worry about, you know, people seeing you or about your fur getting messy?'

'I've been a bit of a fool,' said Scoobie  softly, looking down at the ground. It wasn't easy for her to admit that she'd been wrong. It's not something cats normally do and none of them have much practice at it. 'I thought I was special,' she said. 'Just because I had my picture on a calendar.'

'But you are special,' said Jeremy.

Scoobie looked up, expectantly. 'Do you think so?' she asked. 'It was only a photograph on a calendar.'

'Not because of that,' said Sadie, dismissively.

'No.' said Toby. 'You're special because you're you. You'll always be special to us.'

Scoobie felt her heart swell. She was so happy she wanted to cry.

'We thought we'd climb a tree this afternoon,' said Betty. 'We've never climbed the north side of the oak at the bottom of my garden.'

'It'll be a bit of a challenge,' said Jeremy.

'I'd love to try it!' said Scoobie.

'Great!' said Toby. 'It was going to be a special sort of day anyway. Having you back with us will make it a really extra special day.'

And it was.

When Scoobie went back home that evening, after a tremendous adventure climbing the north side of Betty's oak tree, she felt happy for the first time in months. She didn't even bother to look up at the calendar on the wall.

Moral

If you stand in your own shadow, your world will be dim and your vision will be limited.

The Gentle Art Of Sitting
On A Lap

You couldn't find two cats who had less in common than Tinker and Charlotte.

Tinker was 17 years old and weighed as much as a small child. When he moved about (which he did not do any more often than hunger and nature required) he did so like a tanker: slow, steady and seemingly unstoppable. Even as a kitten he had been large and rather slow. Nimble was not a word anyone had ever applied to him. Tinker had two subsidiary interests (eating and sleeping) but laps were the love of his life. Tinker liked sitting on laps in the same way that small boys like penknives and little girls like dolls. Tinker loved laps of all kinds. Thin ones, fat ones, smooth ones, lumpy ones, still ones, jerky ones — he loved them all. The Uprights with whom he lived never grumbled about Tinker's apparent lack of drive or ambition and never wanted him to do anything else other than to be a lap cat. They enjoyed having him on their laps.

Charlotte, ten years younger, was dainty,

slim and graceful. While Tinker moved about like a tanker she danced around the house and garden like a dinghy bobbing about on a storm troubled sea. She was incapable of moving slowly and as unlikely as a butterfly to move steadily in one direction. She looked delicate and fragile but this was misleading. She was, in truth, a feisty and mischievous cat who loved nothing better than climbing up trees and chasing birds (though, in her defence it has to be said that she never actually caught any).

She was proud of her ability to climb any tree she could find. She constantly looked astonished, as though the entire world had been deliberately designed to surprise her.

'Let's go for a run in the garden!' Charlotte would say to Tinker. 'The sun is shining. It's a beautiful day. Let's race up a tree.'

Tinker would open one eye and look at her. 'Why would we want to race up a tree?' he would ask. 'What will we do when we get to the top?'

'Race back down again, of course!' answered Charlotte, as though the answer was so obvious that only a complete idiot would ask the question.

'I don't want to race anywhere,' Tinker would tell Charlotte, for the millionth time. 'I'm a lap cat. That's what I like doing and that's what I'm good at.' He would sigh deeply, shudder lightly at the very idea of such pointless and exhausting activity, close the eye which he had so reluctantly wasted energy in opening, and go back to sleep. He didn't think badly of Charlotte. He didn't wonder why she was wasting her life racing about with such a transparent lack of purpose. It never occurred to him to think that she might be better off learning how to sit on a lap. Some cats climb trees and some lie on laps. And that, thought Tinker, was simply that.

He did try to explain.

He explained that there is more to sitting on a lap than meets the eye. He pointed out that cats who sit on laps (and do it well) are forging a strong link between cats and Uprights. He told her that it is just as difficult to sit on a lap properly as it is to climb a tree. It is, he pointed out, a little bit an art and a little bit a science. And he bemoaned the fact the way that young cats look down on sitting on laps.

'It's a dying art,' he said. 'You have to mould yourself to the lap; you have to move when the lap moves; you have to stay still when the lap is still; you have to be forever alert to the possibility that the owner of the lap may want to terminate the sitting; and you have to know how to teach the owner of the lap how to get the best out of you.' He sighed and licked his chest for a moment. 'You young cats just want to be off out all the time,' he said. There was a long sad pause. 'You simply don't understand about laps.'

It was all a waste of time, of course. Charlotte didn't understand, didn't want to understand and wasn't impressed by his arguments. And eventually she got tired of asking Tinker to climb trees or run around the garden. Slowly, she realised that he was not a 'climbing trees' sort of cat. And slowly, and rather sadly, she began to think less of him.

It didn't happen overnight, of course.

But it happened.

She began to look at him rather critically and she found herself wondering what sort of cat would waste his life doing nothing but sit on laps.

She wasn't the sort of cat who naturally thought badly of other cats. She regarded herself as being broad-minded and generally uncritical. She was, she thought, a liberal sort of cat, prepared to live and let live without imposing her own beliefs and preferences on others.

But when it came to Tinker she had something of a blind spot. She simply couldn't understand how a perfectly healthy cat could deliberately allow himself to waste his days sitting on laps. It didn't seem right. And as the days and weeks and months went by it troubled her more and more.

And eventually she began to despise him.

She looked down her pretty little nose at him and if she had known what a sneer was, or had ever learned how to sneer, she would have sneered at him.

Tinker knew, of course.

He had been around a long time and it wasn't the first time he'd been the object of another cat's inadequately concealed contempt.

But, although he'd never really minded before, this time it did hurt. He liked Charlotte a lot. He thought she was fun and kind and warm-hearted and bright and generous and loyal and, generally speaking, a *good cat*. (There was no higher praise in Tinker's mind, than to describe another feline as a *good cat*.) He regarded Charlotte as the sort of cat he would have been proud to have had as a daughter, if he'd ever had the time to spare away from learning how to sit on laps.

He wanted to explain to her that he was every bit as proud of his skills as a lap cat as she was proud of her skills at climbing trees. He wanted her to understand because he liked her. But he didn't know what to say to convince her and so he said nothing. And instead of saying something he nursed his sadness deep inside him where it developed into an ache in his heart.

And as his sadness grew so his pride and self-belief slowly shrank. Within a very short space of time he had lost the confidence it had taken him a lifetime to find. He began to wonder if he really had been wasting his life. Maybe he should have spent his years climbing trees.

And then Charlotte injured her leg.

She fell from a branch thirty feet up a beech tree in a neighbour's garden and it took her two hours to drag herself back home again afterwards. She couldn't manage to drag herself through the cat flap and was in a terrible state when the Upright in Trousers found her lying on the step outside the back door. They took her straight to the vet who kept her in his hospital for several days. For a while the Uprights didn't think she would survive.

'You must keep her indoors for two weeks,' instructed the vet, when they were told that they could collect her. The vet was a kindly man who wore a three piece tweed suit and a large droopy moustache. 'Put a litter tray down for her and keep her in the house. If she rests then the break will heal but if she damages that leg any more she'll be crippled for life.'

Charlotte didn't like being kept indoors.

She knew it was for her own good. But that didn't make it any easier.

On the second day of her convalescence Charlotte's Upright in Trousers picked her up and sat down on the sofa next to the Upright who wears a Skirt with Charlotte on his lap. Tinker was already drowsing on the lap of the Upright who wears a Skirt.

Charlotte curled herself up into a ball and tried to relax. It was nice to be lying on something warm. Once, a long time ago, she'd heard Tinker describe lying on a lap as having 'underfur heating'.

But, somehow, it wasn't quite as pleasant as she'd hoped it would be. And however much she wriggled she just couldn't quite manage to get comfy. She got up, turned round (with some difficulty, partly because of the uneven nature of the Upright's lap and partly because of her injury) and lay down again. It wasn't any better.

'Just try and let yourself go,' whispered Tinker.

Charlotte looked across at him. She'd assumed he was asleep.

'Don't try so hard,' suggested Tinker softly. 'Allow yourself to mould to the lap, rather than trying to get the lap to fit you.'

'There's a great gap in the middle,' complained Charlotte.

'Of course there is!' said Tinker, with a smile in his voice. 'But if you let yourself fit the lap you'll soon be very comfortable.'

Charlotte tried very hard. But, to her astonishment, it wasn't as easy as she'd assumed it would be.

'I keep thinking I'm going to fall,' she said.

'You won't,' Tinker assured her. 'The

Upright will automatically adjust to stop you falling.'

'But I *might* fall!'

'Look down,' said Tinker. 'How far is it to the carpet?'

'Two feet at the most.'

'Exactly,' said Tinker gently. 'Even with your bad leg a fall of two feet isn't going to kill you.'

'I suppose not,' agreed Charlotte, rather reluctantly.

'You won't fall,' said Tinker. 'But you can't make the lap fit you. It's up to you to make your body fit the Upright's lap.'

'Are all laps like this?' asked Charlotte.

'No,' said Tinker. 'Every lap is different.'

'They're all different?' cried Charlotte, horrified. 'How on earth do you manage to fit onto laps so easily if they're all different?'

'Experience,' said Tinker calmly. 'When you've sat on a few laps you'll soon get the hang of it.'

There was silence for a while as Charlotte struggled to adapt herself to the Upright's uneven lap. Eventually she managed to get into a position which enabled her to relax just a little.

'It's not as easy as I thought,' said Charlotte softly.

'I don't expect it's as hard as climbing

trees,' said Tinker.

There was silence for a while.

'To be honest I think it's much harder,' confessed Charlotte. 'I don't know how you make it look so easy.'

She did as Tinker had suggested and relaxed into the Upright's lap. Slowly, she began to feel more comfortable. And she began to purr with satisfaction.

Tinker said nothing. But inside his chest the heart ache melted away just as the winter snows disappear in the growing warmth of springtime. He was relieved to have won respect from Charlotte. But he was also pleased to have gained back his self-respect.

Moral

It doesn't matter what you do.
What matters is how proud you are
of what you do.

No Time To Smell
The Flowers

Hyacinth and Mimi lived in a large suburban house with two large Uprights and three small ones. Hyacinth was a multi-coloured tortoiseshell and Mimi was a white short haired Persian. They were both very beautiful and they both knew that they were both very beautiful.

They were also both very fond of fresh mouse.

They were well looked after and well fed by their Uprights. If you'd asked them, neither of them would have been able to produce a single complaint. Meals were served twice a day on fresh plates. And their Uprights never offered them anything but the very best food available. When they had fish it was trout or salmon. When they had meat it was fresh chicken or turkey. Occasionally, they were given duck. When they were given food out of a tin they were given the most expensive brand an up-market supermarket could provide.

But, as Hyacinth once said, you simply can't beat an occasional fresh mouse.

The two cats looked after their mousal needs themselves.

'If I'm going to eat a mouse I like to know it's one I've caught myself,' said Hyacinth. 'I like to keep my paw in. You never know when you might need to catch your own food on a regular basis.'

But they hunted in very different ways.

Hyacinth went out hunting only when she felt like a fresh mouse. This was usually no more than two, or perhaps three, times a week. 'It's enough to keep my paw in,' she said. 'And I don't really want to eat fresh mouse more than two or three times a week.' On the days when she didn't go hunting Hyacinth would laze around. On sunny days she would find a pleasant spot in the garden and bask in the sunshine. On cold days she would curl up beside a radiator.

Mimi, on the other hand, was a very busy cat. She went hunting every day. And since she was very good at hunting she nearly always returned home with a mouse to eat.

She caught so many mice that even though she ate two or three a day (and sometimes ate so many that she made herself quite uncomfortably ill) she simply couldn't eat everything she caught.

'I'm getting a bit fed up of fresh mouse,' she confessed to Hyacinth one day.

Hyacinth stared at her in horror. 'Fed up of fresh mouse?' she cried. 'Why?'

'I catch too many,' explained Mimi. 'And when I've caught them I don't like to waste them.'

'Then why not go hunting less often?' asked Hyacinth. 'If you hunted less often, and caught less mice, you wouldn't feel the need to eat so many. You'd enjoy your hunting more. You'd enjoy your mice meals far more. You wouldn't run the risk of ridding the neighbourhood of mice. (This was a real fear of Hyacinth's, though she hadn't liked to mention it before.) And you certainly wouldn't be fed up of fresh mouse.'

Mimi, whose best friends would not have described her as a great intellectual, thought about this for a while. 'You know, Hyacinth,' she said eventually. 'I think you're right.'

'You've been busy for no reason,' said Hyacinth. 'Take time out to smell the grass and the flowers and you'll enjoy life far more.'

And that's exactly what Mimi did. She might not have been the brightest cat in the neighbourhood. But she wasn't stupid either. And she knew that what Hyacinth said made sense.

Moral

It's not enough to be busy.
The big question is:
what are you busy about?

The Sun Cat

Pickles was a sun worshipper.

He enjoyed chasing birds, catching mice, climbing trees and doing all the other things other cats like doing. He was perfectly normal in that respect.

But lying in the sun was his favourite activity.

Pickles, who liked to describe himself as the Sun Cat, had, over the years, discovered that there were five really good spots for sun bathing. Each of the five had its own special advantage.

Here is the list:

1. On the rocking chair in the bay window of the Uprights' bedroom.

This spot was good for mornings only since in the afternoons the sun was always on the other side of the house. This was Pickles' favourite spot during winter mornings when it was far too cold to be sitting outside.

2. In the middle of the thick rug in the living room.

Pickles had, over, the years, discovered that there was one spot on this rug which kept the sun from early afternoon until sunset. As long as there was some sunshine filtering through the net curtains it really didn't matter to Pickles how cold or windy it was outside.

3. On the wickerwork chair in the conservatory.

There was no heating in the conservatory so this spot wasn't much use during the winter months. But it had always been good for sunbathing during early spring or late autumn and as far as Pickles was concerned it had improved from 'good' to 'excellent' after the Uprights had put a couple of cushions on the wickerwork chair. The big advantage with this spot was that because of the position of the conservatory it was perfectly possible to sunbathe in one position for the whole day.

4. On the paved patio outside the dining room windows.

Pickles had been quite young when he had discovered that paving slabs absorb and retain the heat from the sun. He knew that this phenomenon meant that lying on hard paving isn't necessarily as unpleasant as one might imagine it to be. Once he had settled down in the sun Pickles usually liked to stay where he was. He was an enthusiastic believer in energy conservation and wasn't keen on unnecessary activity of any kind. But hard paving slabs are hard paving slabs and even Pickles found that he needed to move around a little from time to time. The good thing about warm paving slabs was that it meant that Pickles could move about from one warm spot to another warm spot. This was Pickles' favourite spot in the early morning (when there was still dew on the grass), after summer showers, on cool days when there was a slight breeze and on Sunday mornings when the Upright in Trousers cut the grass (and invariably made a great deal of additional noise shouting at the machine with which he cut it).

5. On the lawn.

Pickles was not a cat who liked to lie in the shade and there were surprisingly few places on the lawn which were good for day-long sunbathing. The perfect spot, Pickles had found, was six feet north of the vegetable patch and five feet to the left of the chrysanthemum bed. This was where Pickles spent the greater part of every day during late spring, summer and early autumn. He liked sunbathing on grass. It felt soft and smelt good and if you woke up and needed a little light entertainment there were always plenty of small insects rushing around as though their lives depended on it.

The one thing missing from this list was, of course, somewhere to sunbathe when there was no sun.

This was something that had been a worry to Pickles for as long as he could remember.

And, as the years went by, he got no closer to finding a solution.

Until one day in January.

It was raining hard, as it had been doing for what seemed like weeks, and the sun was nowhere to be seen. It was, in fact, nearly a month since Pickles had seen anything remotely resembling a sunbeam — and even then it had been thin, watery and insipid and had borne very little resemblance to the real thing.

Pickles, needless to say, was feeling rather glum and was moping about the house struggling to find somewhere to settle. He'd spent half an hour outside a hole in the skirting board because he'd felt sure he'd heard a mouse inside. But nothing had emerged. He'd tried to climb into the airing cupboard but a pile of towels had fallen off a shelf and nearly knocked him out. He'd gone out into the garden for two minutes and come back through the cat flap at full speed. It had taken him twenty minutes to lick the wet soil off his paws. He hated wet soil almost as much as he loved the sun.

He had tried taking a nap on the thick rug in the living room. But without the sun it seemed rather sad and pointless.

In fact, without the sun, everything seemed rather sad and pointless.

And so he continued to mope around the

house looking for something to do or somewhere to sit.

Eventually he found himself in the small room that the Upright in Trousers used as a study. It wasn't a room that Pickles usually bothered with. There was a desk, a chair, a bookcase, a filing cabinet and a telephone. Not much else.

Pickles jumped up onto the desk. There were some papers there, neatly sorted into three piles. He lay down on the middle and largest pile. It was pleasant enough. But not exactly satisfying. He looked up. There was a table lamp on the desk. He reached up and touched it. To his surprise the lamp moved. He touched it again. It moved back to where it had been. It seemed to be held up by a simple system of arms and springs. He sat up as high as he could and tapped the lamp again. He could, he realised move it to wherever he wanted. He looked down. There was a small white button fitted to the base of the lamp. He tapped the button.

SUNSHINE!

Suddenly the desk was flooded with sunshine.

Bright, warm sunshine.

Pickles couldn't believe it.

He looked up. The lamp was shining brightly down onto the desk. Onto him.

He tapped the button again.

The sunshine went. Instantly. One minute it was there. The next minute it had gone.

He tapped the button.

SUNSHINE!

He reached up and moved the lamp, positioning it carefully so that the pool of sunshine centred on the papers in the middle of the desk.

He lay down and closed his eyes.

This was just like summer.

Now Pickles had a sixth spot for sunbathing. And he had round the year sunshine.

Moral

The sun is always shining somewhere in your life — if you're prepared to look for it.

The Wisdom Of A Kitten

Snowflake was the prettiest cat anyone (including her) had ever seen. She was quite matter-of-fact about this and not in the slightest bit conceited.

Her prettiness was just a fact of life and as far as she was concerned there was as little point in being vain about it as there would have been in her being jealous if she'd ever come across a cat who was prettier (something which, she felt, was fairly unlikely but which she didn't automatically rule out).

Snowflake would have happily traded all her good looks to be able to consider herself a 'clever' cat.

She regarded beauty as something that was very superficial. What she really wanted was to be able to consider herself to be a wise cat. Not necessarily a clever cat, for that, she realised, is something quite different. But a wise cat.

To be a wise cat, she thought, would be something of which a cat could justifiably be proud.

Everywhere she went she would listen carefully to what other cats had to say in the

69

hope that one day she would learn the secret of wisdom. She was so keen to learn the secret that she would even listen to Uprights talking — even though every cat knows that wisdom is not a trait usually found among Uprights.

'How can I become wise?' she asked an elderly tomcat whom she met in an alleyway near to her home.

'Why are you asking me?' the tomcat asked her.

'Because you are old,' she told him. (Cats, it should be noted, are not sensitive about their age in the way that Uprights can sometimes be. Indeed, most cats regard a great age as something of which to be proud.)

'You are making a mistake in assuming that wisdom necessarily comes with age,' said the tomcat. 'If I was wise do you think I would still be skulking around in alleyways looking for fights?'

'How do I become wise?' she asked an old Persian who lived two doors away.

'What makes you think that I know the answer to that question?' asked the old Persian.

'You always seem very wise,' replied Snowflake.

'That's because I never say very much,' said the Persian. 'To be honest I'm really quite stupid. But I realised that if I never said anything much then other cats would not realise just how stupid I am.' She sighed. 'To my surprise what happened was that cats mistook my silence for wisdom.'

Every time she asked her question Snowflake seemed to get no closer to the answer.

In the end she obtained the answer to her question from the unlikeliest of sources.

She was beginning to despair of ever discovering the missing secret when, while walking in a garden near to her home one day, she looked for somewhere to take cover from an unexpected shower of rain. The only place to shelter was a small garden shed. The door was open, so she popped inside. Hearing a sound she looked around and saw a little black and white kitten edging towards the door.

'Where are you going?' asked Snowflake.

'Just leaving,' said the kitten, obviously nervous.

'Why?' demanded Snowflake. 'It's still raining.'

'This is a very small shed and you're much bigger than I am,' replied the kitten.

'And you thought I might object to sharing it with you?'

'I'd rather get wet than end up in a fight

with you,' said the kitten. 'If I get wet I'll soon dry out. But if I end up in a fight I'll definitely come off worst.'

Snowflake smiled. 'Please stay,' she said. 'I don't want to fight you.' She thought for a moment, struck by the good sense of the kitten's reply. 'You seem very wise for such a young kitten,' she said.

'Thank you,' said the kitten. 'But I really don't think I'm wise at all.'

'I think you're very modest,' said Snowflake. 'Will you tell me what made you do and say what you just did and said?'

'Oh that's easy,' replied the kitten. 'I always ask myself what a smart cat would do. Then I do that.'

Moral

The wise cat isn't necessarily the wisest cat, but may just be the cat who does what the wisest cat would do.

The Cat Who Didn't Like Heights

Columbus stood on the branch and looked down. He felt dizzy and distinctly unwell. He hated heights. Not for the first time he asked himself what he was doing up a tree. Despite his name, Columbus was not a great explorer.

'Let's go up higher!' said Horace. Horace was a ginger tomcat who was the undisputed leader of their small gang.

'I don't think we can go much higher,' said Willy, rather nervously. Willy, a black and white cat was, like Columbus, a born follower. Like Columbus he was only up the tree because Horace had said that was what they were going to do.

'This is a very nice height,' said Columbus, who would much rather have been at home sitting by the fire.

'Don't be wimpy!' said Horace. He looked up. 'We can get much higher.'

'Why do we want to go higher?' asked Columbus. 'The view from here is really very good.' He risked another peep down but quickly closed his eyes. He was now getting

73

very worried about how he was going to get down the tree.

'Why?' snarled Horace. 'Why? Because we can. Because it's exciting. Because there are more branches up there. Because if we don't we'll be wimps. Because I say we should.' He reached up with his front paws, dug his claws into the tree's bark and sprang upwards from the branch he was standing on. Moments later he was perched on a branch another eight feet above their heads. 'Come on!' he called. 'The view from up here is even better.'

'I'm coming,' said Willy. He sounded terrified and clearly didn't want to go any higher. He turned to Columbus. 'Are you coming?'

Columbus looked at Willy and knew that the fear and anxiety he could see in Willy's eyes had to be clearly visible in his own too. He was scared. Why, he asked himself, was he doing this? Why was he scrambling up a tree he didn't want to climb? Why was he putting himself through so much misery? What was the purpose?

During the last year he'd been in similar situations many times before but these were not questions he'd ever thought to ask himself before.

But now that he was asking himself the questions he felt he had to find some answers.

And the only answer he could come up with was 'fear'.

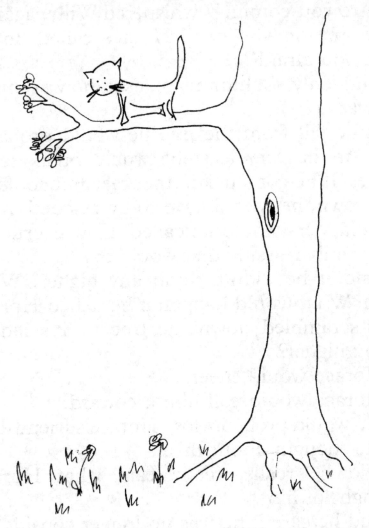

He had climbed forty feet up a tree, and was preparing to go even higher, because he was afraid of what Horace would have said if he'd stayed on the ground.

He was afraid of what Horace would think of him. He was more afraid of what Horace would think of him than he was of falling from the tree.

'Are you coming?' whispered Willy, again.

'Come on you two!' Horace called down. 'Are you afraid?'

Suddenly, Columbus realised how stupid it all was.

If he fell from the tree he would probably die. At the very least he would break some bones. If he got stuck in the tree, and couldn't get down, he would have to be rescued. Men with ladders would be called. How excruciatingly embarrassing that would be.

And if he didn't climb any higher? What then? What would happen if he defied Horace and scrambled down the tree — instead of going higher?

Horace would sneer.

Horace would call him a coward.

He would probably lose Horace's friendship.

He thought about this.

Did he really, really care what Horace thought of him?

Did he care if he was no longer considered suitable to be a member of Horace's small gang?

No.

He didn't care what Horace thought. He really didn't.

'Come on you two cowards!' called Horace, looking down from his perch way, way above them.

'I'm going down now,' Columbus called back. He thought about adding that he was hungry or bored. But he didn't. Just that he was going down.

'Are you really?' asked Willy. 'Going down?'

'Yes.'

'I think I'll come with you.'

Slowly, hesitantly, carefully, Columbus began to edge backwards down the tree. He tried not to look down too much. Above him Willy followed.

'Where are you two going?' yelled Horace. 'What are you doing? We're supposed to be climbing a tree!'

They ignored him.

'I don't want you in my gang any more,' said Horace.

They carried on climbing backwards down the tree. The nearer they got to the ground the better Columbus felt.

'Without us he hasn't got a gang,' said Willy quietly.

Columbus laughed a little to himself. He felt better than he'd felt for months. He felt free again. Free to do what he wanted to do.

'My Uprights have got a log fire,' he said to Willy. 'Would you like to come in and have a nap in front of it? I'm sure they won't mind.'

'I'd like that,' said Willy. 'I'd like that very much.'

High up in the tree they could hear Horace. He was still busily berating them.

Columbus felt good.

When he got back home maybe the Upright in a Skirt would put out a saucer of milk. And maybe a little fish.

Moral

Only when you know why you do things will you know whether they are worth doing. (Sometimes the question to ask is 'Why?' At other times the question to ask is 'Why not?' The trick is knowing which of these questions is the right one to ask.)

Princess Graceful And
The Prince Of Charms

Roger and Martha Wilson were people who liked to be in control. He worked as a partner at a firm of solicitors in very posh offices in a very smart district of London. He specialised in international corporate law and charged fees that would have made a banker blush. She was an interior decorator with a flourishing business of her own. She wouldn't even consider decorating anything less than a castle, a chateau or a twelve room apartment in the swishest part of town. Their clients were almost as rich and successful as they were.

They both got up at six every morning.

He had breakfast, exercised in their private gym and was picked up by a chauffeur-driven car at eight sharp. The morning's newspapers (*Financial Times, Wall Street Journal, International Herald Tribune, Times* and *Daily Telegraph*) were laid in a neat pile on the back seat so that by the time he reached his office at nine he would have read his way through them all.

After swimming thirty laps in their private pool she spent thirty minutes with her private trainer and then thirty minutes with her personal hairdresser/beautician. She left for her nearby office at 9.30 am. She drove herself in a yellow Porsche. By the time she got to her office her personal assistant would have sifted and sorted the day's mail and the overnight faxes and e-mails.

In the evenings they both arrived home at seven unless they had a 'do' to attend in the city in which case they would meet at their pied à terre where they would bathe, change and be ready for whatever excitements the evening held for them.

Their main house was run, with Teutonic efficiency, by a French housekeeper, a Swedish maid and a Belgian gardener (who was married to the French housekeeper and having an affair with the Swedish maid). In the city they relied on the concierge service in the building where they had their pied à terre.

Everything in their lives ran smoothly and methodically. Even dental and medical emergencies were slotted into their days with great efficiency. Domestic problems (malfunctioning boiler, blocked chimney, unhappy washing machine) were all dealt with in their absence by their staff. The chauffeur kept their car serviced and one of Mr Wilson's personal assistants made sure that all the paperwork (insurance and so on) that might otherwise have blighted their lives was dealt with on their behalf.

Only two things in their lives weren't under their constant and perfect control.

And those weren't things.

They were the Princess Graceful II and the Prince of Charms III.

The Princess Graceful II and the Prince of Charms III were seven-year-old Burmese cats and they recognised no earthly master or mistress.

For the first five years that they shared a world together Mr and Mrs Wilson had attempted to impose some discipline on their cats.

'Come here!' Mr Wilson would say.

'Sit there!' Mrs Wilson would say.

'Don't do that!' Mr Wilson would command.

'Don't lie there!' Mrs Wilson would command.

They might as well have been ordering the wind to blow.

The Princess Graceful II and the Prince of Charms III ignored every instruction they were given.

Naturally, Mr and Mrs Wilson found this

almost unbearably difficult to accept.

They were accustomed to getting what they wanted, when they wanted it. Like spoilt children they did not cope easily when they were thwarted.

Their frustration mounted. They were even beginning to consider the awful possibility that the cats would have to go.

Until, one day, Mr Wilson discovered a solution to their problem.

The solicitor and the interior decorator were sitting in their drawing room (white hand-made rugs on a bleached wood floor, white leather sofa, white leather chairs) when the two cats wandered in together (they hardly ever went anywhere without one another).

Slowly, the Princess Graceful II sauntered over to one of the unoccupied chairs. She looked up and prepared to jump.

'Don't . . . ' began Mrs Wilson.

The Princess Graceful II jumped up onto the chair, turned round three times and settled down.

Equally deliberately the Prince of Charms III followed her. He too turned round three times before settling down alongside the Princess Graceful II.

'Please lie on the chair,' said Mr Wilson, quietly.

The cats ignored him completely but his wife looked at him.

He beamed back at her.

'What on earth are you doing?' she demanded. 'You know how I hate them being on the chairs. Their paws are dirty and they moult.'

'But they never take any notice,' said her husband. 'They never do what we tell them to do.'

'Noooo . . . ,' agreed Mrs Wilson. 'That's true.'

'Lie down there and go to sleep,' said Mr Wilson to the two cats.

Mrs Wilson, puzzled, looked at him.

'Now they're going to do what I want them to do!' said Mr Wilson, very pleased with himself.

'But . . . ' began Mrs Wilson.

'This is the answer,' said Mr Wilson, very pleased with himself. 'I'm going to tell them what to do immediately after they've done it. That way I'll be in charge.'

'Oh,' said Mrs Wilson. 'I see what you mean.' She stared across at the two cats.

The Prince of Charms III sat up and licked his back.

'Lick your back,' she said.

'There you are,' said Mr Wilson. 'There's a bit of a time delay but he's doing exactly what you tell him.'

'Oh this is wonderful!' cried Mrs Wilson, delightedly.

And so everything ended very happily.

Moral

The only way to get a cat to do what you want it to do, is to tell it to do what it's just done.

The Good Listener

The two cats were lying together on the grass. From a distance they seemed to be asleep.

But they weren't.

'I've had a really rough few months,' said Jack, a three-year-old black and white cat. He had white socks and a white patch under his throat but otherwise he was completely black.

The other cat didn't say anything but made one of those strange, non-committal noises cats always make when they don't have anything to say but they want to make it clear that they are listening and prepared to be sympathetic. It sounded a bit like 'Hgm.'

'First of all my Uprights had the whole house painted,' said Jack. 'Do you have any idea how awful that is? The smell. The disturbance. Uprights — complete strangers — wandering every where. The noise. Constant noise. They put the radio on when they arrive and they leave it switched on all day.'

'Hgm,' said the other cat.

'It wasn't as if they just did the outside,' said Jack. 'That would have been bad enough, heaven knows. But they did the inside too. Every room in the house. Even the airing cupboard. For weeks I didn't eat anything that didn't taste of paint. I'll swear that even the mice I caught in the house tasted of paint.'

The other cat nodded slightly.

'I really don't know why they bothered,' said Jack. 'I liked it the way it was before. It was comfortable. It felt lived in. Now everywhere is shiny and bright. We're all terrified of being the first to mark the paintwork.'

The other cat nodded again. 'Hgm,' he said. 'Then there were the visitors. I hate visitors. There were four of them. Two big ones and two small ones. I hate the small ones most.

More noise. We had two weeks of peace after the painters left. Then the visitors came. They stayed for a week. Seven whole days of purgatory. The two small ones seemed to think it was their role in life to chase me round the house. Every time I found somewhere quiet for a snooze I was woken up.' Jack shivered at the memory. 'It was awful,' he said.

'Hgm,' murmured the other cat, sympathetically.

'Then they bought a dog.'

'Hgm hgm,' said the other cat, more audibly this time.

'A dog! One of those wretched little yappy things. Yap yap yap yap yap. Day and night. I don't think it even stops yapping when it eats. It certainly yaps when it's asleep because I've seen it. Why would they buy something like that? Why would they want something like that in the house? Are they mad?' Jack sighed. 'A yappy dog,' he said. 'Decorators, visitors and a yappy dog.'

'Hgm,' said the other cat.

'Still, it could be worse,' said Jack. 'They aren't likely to have the place decorated again for a year or two. They were as fed up with the visitors as I was. And the dog is terrified of me. Every time he sees me he runs away. I scratched his nose and he didn't like it. Yappy dogs are all the same. Lots of bark and no real bite to them.'

'Hgm,' agreed the other cat.

'I feel a bit better now we've talked about things,' said Jack. He paused. 'You've been a great help. Having a chat about things does help, doesn't it?'

'Hgm,' said the other cat.

'Thanks,' said Jack. 'I really appreciate it.'

Moral

Listening is one of the most potent forms of communication.

The Big Mouse Hunt

Charlie, Slinkie and Buster did everything together. Charlie was a six-year-old black and white cat with an affection for fishing, sleeping in front of log fires and chasing leaves. Slinkie was a five-year-old mackerel tabby who loved tinned salmon, moonlight and long walks in long grass. Buster was a seven-year-old marmalade cat who liked to pretend he was much tougher than he was. (He was, if the truth be told, one of the softest, shyest, nicest cats anyone could ever imagine meeting.)

The three of them lived, together with the Uprights who cared for them, in smart terraced houses in a small country market town. The houses in which they lived had very small gardens but since all the gardens in the area were separated from one another by low fences none of the three cats had any difficulty at all in visiting one another and exploring the gardens belonging to the Uprights who had not yet been fortunate enough to find themselves looking after cats.

There were plenty of things to do in the neighbourhood.

When the weather was fine they sometimes spent their days lazing by a stream which ran along the bottom of the gardens. Or they spent time fishing in a goldfish pond belonging to a rather excitable old doctor. Sometimes they jumped across the stream (it was very narrow in several places) and had adventures wandering around on the school playing fields on the other side of the water. Or, if they were feeling less energetic, they just lazed around and told one another tall stories about past adventures (real and imaginary).

When the weather was poor they found their fun indoors. (These were not tough cats. They didn't like being outside in cold or wet weather.) There were plenty of sheds, summerhouses and garages where they could meet. One of their favourite haunts was an old barn which was used to store mowers, rollers, white line markers and other paraphernalia kept by the groundsman who looked after the playing fields. The barn had, over the years, been used to store all sorts of interesting things — including a good deal of grass seed — and it was, therefore, a permanent home for a large number of mice. (There were, indeed, so many mice living there that some senior rodents had asked serious questions about the level of overcrowding.)

It was in the barn, one wet Wednesday afternoon, that the three of them met Tony, a young and rather fiery Siamese who was proud of the fact that his parents had both been Best in Class winners at several important regional cat shows.

Tony was already there when they arrived.

'What do you want?' he demanded, showing them his teeth and making sure his hackles raised. 'This is my hunting ground.'

'Hello!' said Charlie, bravely refusing to show just how nervous he felt. He introduced himself and his two companions. 'We come here often but I haven't seen you here before,' he added, tactfully disputing Tony's territorial claim without actually doing so.

'I moved into the area last Saturday,' said Tony. He told them his name. 'My parents were both Best in Class winners at several important regional cat shows.'

'Have you caught anything yet?' asked Buster.

'Almost,' answered Tony. 'Just before you came I nearly caught an enormous one. Biggest one I've ever seen. I was just about to pounce when he ran away. I think he probably heard you coming.'

'Never mind,' said Buster. 'The place is teeming with mice. We'll catch dozens in no time at all.'

'We usually let them go when we've caught

them,' said Charlie. 'Then we can catch them again another time.'

'There's one mouse I've caught nine times,' said Buster. 'We've become quite good chums.'

'How can you be chums with a mouse?' demanded Tony indignantly.

'Oh, you know,' said Buster. 'When you catch someone that often you get to know their little ways. It's easy to grow fond of them. I could never eat him.'

'Sentimental poppycock,' snarled Tony. 'Mice are for eating. I eat all the ones I catch.' Charlie, Slinkie and Buster couldn't think of anything to say to this and so they stayed silent. And the four of them then settled down to wait.

Buster caught his first mouse after just six minutes. The mouse, who'd been hiding behind an old, opened bag of grass seed, made a run for it and underestimated Buster's speed from a standing start.

'Got one!' said Buster, holding onto the mouse with his right front paw.

'That one's mine!' said Tony.

'How do you make that out?' asked Buster.

'I nearly caught that one earlier on,' said Tony. 'Just before you got here.'

'But you didn't catch him!' said Buster.

'I would have done if you hadn't turned up,' argued Tony.

'OK,' sighed Buster, who just over an hour or so earlier had enjoyed a big lunch of 'meaty chunks in a savoury sauce' and wasn't feeling at all hungry. 'You have him then.' He lifted his paw and moved out of the way to let Tony take over. But Tony was far too slow and the mouse disappeared.

'Your fault!' snarled Tony. 'Clumsy!'

'I thought you'd be quicker than that,' said Buster.

'I'm as quick as anyone here!' snapped back Tony. 'My Great Uncle Blackie was champion ratter at the Bridgend Coal Works in the 1970s. He averaged five kills a night for just under twelve years.'

The four of them settled down again.

This time it was Charlie's turn to catch a mouse.

'That one should have been mine!' said Tony. 'It ran in front of me before you caught it.'

'Exactly,' said Charlie. 'So how does that make it your mouse?'

'You were in my way,' said Tony. 'You interfered with my concentration.'

'OK,' sighed Charlie, anxious to avoid a confrontation. He let Tony take the mouse from him. But moments after the handover the mouse suddenly managed to escape.

'You fool!' cried Tony.

Charlie, astonished, looked at him.

'That was your fault!' said Tony.

For a moment Charlie said nothing. 'Sorry,' he said at last, not because he was really sorry or because he thought that it was his mistake that the mouse had escaped, but because he didn't want an argument to spoil an afternoon's sport. He looked across at Buster and Slinkie who both shrugged elegantly. The shrugs were so understated that Tony wouldn't have understood what they were, or what they meant, even if he had seen them.

Slinkie was the third cat to catch a mouse. She was fast. (Both Charlie and Buster had always agreed that she was the fastest mover they'd ever seen. Faster even than either of them.)

'Don't you lot have any sense of honour?' demanded Tony, very crossly.

Slinkie looked at him. 'What do you mean?'

'That was my mouse!' insisted Tony. He sounded very cross.

Slinkie said nothing, but simply stared at him. She was astonished.

'It was heading in my direction,' said Tony. 'You pinched my mouse.'

Slinkie looked at him, to see if he was joking. He wasn't. 'OK.' she said. 'It's your mouse.'

'It's too late now,' said Tony with a sniff.

For a moment there was silence. Charlie, Slinkie and Buster said nothing. Not even a purr. They couldn't think of anything to say.

'Didn't you say you had to be back home early tonight?' Buster asked Slinkie.

'No . . . ,' began Slinkie. 'Oh, yes,' she said, correcting herself. 'You're right. Thanks for reminding me.'

'I'll come with you,' said Buster.

'Me too,' said Charlie.

'We'll leave you to it, then,' Buster said to Tony.

'Right,' said Tony.

'Happy hunting,' said Slinkie.

'I expect I'll do very well,' Tony said. 'My Great Uncle you know. It's in the blood.'

'Of course,' said Buster.

The three friends tiptoed out of the barn and left Tony sitting beside a hole in the floor. Once outside they ran as fast as they could for the stream.

'What an awful cat!' said Buster.

'I've never heard anything like it!' said Slinkie. 'He took everything we caught.'

'I bet he's never caught a mouse of his own in his life,' said Charlie.

The other two agreed that, despite Tony's ancestry, this was extremely likely.

'But he tried to take all the mice we

95

caught,' said Buster.

'I don't care,' said Slinkie. 'He was welcome to them.'

'Slinkie is right,' said Charlie.

'He was the loser,' said Buster. 'He could have had three new friends.'

'I'd rather have a couple of good chums than all the mice in the world,' said Charlie.

The other two nodded their agreement.

'I'd rather have a couple of good chums than all the mice in the world,' said Charlie

Moral

Real wealth is measured in friendships — not in mice.

Climb The Impossible Dream

Peter was eight-years-old. For seven years he had lived with his Uprights in a beautiful house in the country. The house had a lovely garden and in the middle of the garden there stood a magnificent old oak tree.

For every one of those seven years Peter had dreamt of climbing the old tree. He dreamt of climbing it when he was lying on the rug in front of the fire. He dreamt of climbing it when he was tucked up in the airing cupboard. He dreamt of climbing it when he was sleeping on a comfortable lap. He dreamt of climbing it when he was snoozing in the conservatory.

It was his constant dream. His ambition. His hope. His aspiration.

In his favourite dream he would get right to the very top of the tree; up where the crows and the pigeons stood and chattered away. He would stand on the topmost branch and look down on the house and the garden where he lived. He loved that dream.

Several times he had actually tried to climb the tree.

But he had never been successful.

In fact, to be honest, he had never even got as far as the first branch.

The problem was that the lowest branch was twelve feet off the ground. And the trunk was remarkably smooth and straight.

Peter had tried taking a run at the tree and then racing up it as fast as his legs would carry him; hoping that speed and strong claws would enable him to overcome gravity.

But every attempt had ended in dismal failure.

He'd never even got half way to that first branch.

One day he told Clancy about his dream.

'You'll never climb it,' said Clancy, his best friend. 'It's impossible.'

But Peter refused to believe him.

'The trunk is too straight and there's too much of it,' said Clancy. 'You'd have to be a squirrel to get up there.'

In his mind Peter knew that Clancy was right.

But in his heart he wouldn't accept that he'd never succeed.

'It's my dream,' he told Clancy. 'One day . . . maybe. Perhaps I'll do it one day.'

For a moment Clancy thought of telling his friend to abandon his impossible dream. But then he looked at Peter's face and he stopped himself.

'What right have I to take away my friend's dream?' he asked himself.

'One day,' he agreed, even though in both his heart and his mind he knew that the tree was impossible to climb.

'One day I'll climb it,' said Peter.

'One day you will,' said Clancy.

Peter turned to him and smiled. 'Do you think so?' he asked.

'Absolutely!' said Clancy.

'Thank you,' said Peter softly. 'It makes me feel good to hear you say that.'

Moral

**You don't have to realise your dreams to enjoy them.
All you have to do is keep them alive.**

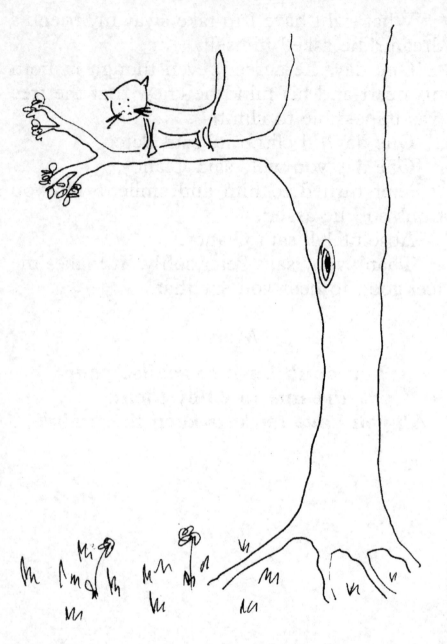

Peter had never even got as far as the first branch

The Price Of Everything And The Value Of Nothing

Two cats were walking down the road. They were both new to the neighbourhood. One was very well-groomed and wore an expensive collar. The other was rather unkempt and had no collar. He had a mouse in his mouth. They stopped for a moment to introduce themselves.

'I'm His Highness Rupert Braunton the 5th,' said the cat with the expensive collar. 'I cost £500. How much did you cost?'

The unkempt cat put down the mouse he was carrying. But he didn't answer.

'How much did you cost?' demanded His Highness.

'I'm not sure,' replied the cat without the collar. 'My name is Fred.'

'I bet you didn't cost anything,' said His Highness with a sneer. 'With a name like Fred I suspect that your Uprights were probably paid to look after you.'

Fred didn't say anything.

'I'm insured for more than £500,' said His Highness. 'My Uprights think I'm more valuable than that now.'

'Oh,' said Fred.

'I don't suppose you're insured at all, are you?' said His Highness.

'I don't know,' said Fred, who didn't know what insurance was let alone what it tasted like.

'How much did you cost?' demanded His Highness.
'I'm not sure,' replied the cat without the collar.

'After I won the big cup last month they said my value had doubled,' said His Highness. Fred nodded.

'Where are you off to?' asked His Highness.

'A cat who lives down the road got knocked over by a car last week,' explained Fred. 'Today is his first day out. I thought I'd go and see how he is.' He looked down at the mouse he'd put down. 'I caught him a fresh mouse. I thought he'd like it.'

'What's the cat's name?' asked His Highness.

'Billy,' said Fred. 'His Uprights call him Billy.'

'Billy!' said His Highness. 'Another common name. Was he a stray?'

'I think so,' admitted Fred.

'So he didn't cost anything either?'

'Probably not.'

'No insurance?'

'I don't expect so.'

'How very common,' said His Highness with a sniff.

'Do you want to come with me?' asked Fred. 'We could say the mouse was from both of us?'

His Highness stared at the other cat in astonishment. 'Me visit a cat called Billy? A cat who cost nothing?' He snorted. 'Don't be silly.' And with that he turned round and walked away.

Fred picked up the mouse and continued on his way.

Billy was very pleased to see him. And

delighted with the mouse. He told Fred all about his accident and insisted that they share the mouse for tea.

Moral

***It's not what you cost that matters.
It's what you're worth.***

The Feast

Ruby loved eating. It was her raison d'être. She herself was the first to admit that she lived to eat, rather than the other way round. Her ten favourite foods (in order of preference) were: cold roast chicken, turkey, Stilton, fresh rabbit, custard, Cheddar cheese, mouse, clotted cream, duck and Black Forest gateau.

When she wandered into the kitchen one Saturday evening and found the remains of a large roasted chicken cooling on the kitchen table she could hardly believe her good fortune. From the laughter and chatter coming from the dining room she knew that her Uprights were entertaining, and unlikely to interrupt her for some time to come.

She started with the remains of the chicken breast, ate what was left of a wing and polished off several strips of fatty skin (her favourite part of the bird). She then rested for a few moments before going back to finish the remains of the other wing and clean the meat off as many bones as she could manage.

Afterwards she retired to the airing cupboard to digest her feast.

Sadly, the post prandial process was not uneventful for, although this is a truth which Ruby has always vehemently denied, there are limits to the digestive capacity of even the most gluttonous cat.

It would be impolite, and certainly unnecessary, to go into fine detail of the consequences of the feast; sufficient, perhaps, to point out that Ruby's Upright who wears a skirt had to put a collection of neatly ironed items (including two sheets, four towels, four pillow cases, six shirts, five blouses and a variety of underwear) straight back into the washing machine.

Moral

Too much of a good thing can be too much of a good thing — even if it is at someone else's expense.

The Cat With No Fear

There were four of them and Bertie.

Kenny, Olivia, Philemena and Oscar all readily admitted that they were frightened of the Great Dane which lived at number 47. This had come about because none of them would cross the garden where the Great Dane lived.

Bertie insisted that he had no such fear and to prove that he was not afraid he had raced across the garden not once but twice. The first time had been to the garden belonging to number 45. The second time had been back to the garden at number 49.

'I know no fear,' Bertie said, boldly, when he returned. 'Fear is simply a state of mind. I have trained myself to eradicate such weakness from my personality.'

The others, who between them shared a considerable number of fears, stared at him in amazement and awe.

'You have no fears?' said Kenny.

'None,' said Bertie boldly.

'What about rats?' asked Olivia. 'Surely you are afraid of rats? I hate rats. I can't stand them.' She shivered at the very thought of rats.

'I like rats,' said Bertie. 'They're good sport. The more the better. I once killed six in an hour. Great big, evil looking brutes they were.'

Olivia shivered again. 'Oh dear,' she said. 'Oh me oh my.'

'Aren't you afraid of heights?' asked Philemena.

'Heights?' said Bertie. 'Who's afraid of heights?'

'I am,' admitted Philemena, rather shyly. 'I can't go more than about ten feet up a tree. And I couldn't possibly look out of the bedroom window without feeling queasy.'

'Oh I like heights,' said Bertie. 'Heights don't bother me in the slightest little bit. I once climbed out of a bedroom window, up onto a flat roof and over onto next door's roof. It must have been forty feet above the ground.'

'Crumbs!' said Philemena, who was more impressed than she dared admit.

'I used to be afraid of things,' admitted Bertie. 'When I was a little kitten.' He licked at his chest where a stray hair had slipped out of place. 'But no more. Not for a long time.'

Just then an Upright called. They all turned towards the voice. It was Bertie's Upright who wears a Skirt.

'Bertie!' called the Upright. 'Look who's here!'

The cats all looked more closely. Bertie's Upright who wears a Skirt was accompanied by a second Upright, also in a skirt. The second Upright was larger, much larger, and quite a lot older.

'Yikes!' gulped Bertie. 'Oh no!'

'What's the matter?' asked Philemena.

'It's the Upright they call Aunt Maude!' croaked Bertie. He was shivering and shaking.

'Are you all right?' asked Kenny.

'She's scary!' said Bertie. He shook uncontrollably. 'And she always picks me up and puts me on her lap. She reeks of talcum powder.'

'She looks quite harmless to me,' said Kenny.

'Quite nice, actually,' said Philemena.

'Positively charming!' added Olivia.

'Oh no she's not,' said Bertie. 'You've got to hide me.' He crouched down and slid around behind the other four cats. He closed his eyes and tried to shrink.

The other four cats looked at one another and exchanged smiles. There was nothing malevolent in their enjoyment of his obvious distress. They just couldn't help themselves. (And who could blame them?)

'We'll hide you,' said Oscar, making a supreme effort and keeping all the smiles out of his voice. 'But, first, you have to tell us something.'

'What?' demanded Bertie, whispering. 'What do you want?'

'Are you afraid of Aunt Maude?'

Bertie gulped. 'Yes!' he admitted. 'I'm frightened of her. Now quick — hide me!'

Moral

**No one is fearless.
Everyone is afraid of something.**

The Wisdom Of Fools

Pip and Snowy looked up at where Nippy was sitting on top of the flat roof of the brick-built garden shed.

'Is it safe to go over?' asked Snowy.

Nippy looked down. 'Oh yes,' he answered, immediately.

'The dog's not out in the garden?'

'No.'

'Good,' said Snowy. 'Because I really don't like that dog.' He shivered. The Uprights who owned the garden they were about to enter owned a huge Bull Mastiff. Snowy wasn't particularly fond of dogs of any variety. If God had asked his opinion he would have definitely voted for a dog-free world. But he especially disliked large dogs with strong, sharp teeth. He and Pip leapt up onto the top of the fence and down into the garden on the other side.

Seconds later the dog appeared.

Pip and Snowy didn't have time to look up and protest to Nippy. They scrambled back up and onto the top of the fence. Pip did so with inches to spare. Snowy lost a few hairs from the tip of her tail.

Pip and Snowy looked up at where Nippy was sitting on top of the flat roof of the brick-built garden shed. 'Is it safe to go over?' asked Snowy.

'You said the dog wasn't there!' protested Pip, when he'd got his breath back and his heart had gone back to beating more normally.

'Sorry about that!' said Nippy. 'I didn't think it was there.'

'But why didn't you say that you didn't *think* it was there?' demanded Snowy. She looked at the end of her tail and shook her head sadly. Her tail was her pride and joy. She licked it to try and hide the fact that some hairs were missing. 'You said it wasn't there!' she protested. 'You were quite positive about there being no dog there.'

Nippy looked a little uncomfortable. 'I didn't like to say 'I don't know',' he said.

'Why on earth not?' demanded Snowy.

'Because only fools and wimps say 'I don't know',' replied Nippy.

Pip and Snowy looked at one another and shook their heads sadly.

'Sometimes,' said Snowy, looking up at Nippy, 'sometimes, admitting that you don't know is the only sensible thing to do.'

Moral

Saying 'I don't know' is a sign of wisdom and strength — not a sign of stupidity and weakness.

The Legend

Kitty the kitten was dozing on the porch swing seat when her half sister Lucy woke her up.

'What's up?' asked Kitty, sleepily.

'Wake up!' said Lucy excitedly.

'Have we got chicken?' demanded Kitty, sitting up.

'No, no, much more exciting than that!'

'Fish? Salmon?'

'No. It isn't food at all.'

Kitty lay down, preparing to go back to sleep.

'You must wake up!' said Lucy. 'You'll never guess who I've just seen.'

Kitty sat up again. 'Who?'

'Eddie.'

'Eddie who?'

'The Eddie.'

'What do you mean 'The Eddie'?'

Lucy sighed. 'You know. Eddie. The cat who fought off eight dogs at the Battle of Langham Drive.'

Now Kitty was impressed. Everyone knew who the Eddie was. 'He's here?' she asked.

'Just visiting,' replied Lucy. 'He's got family

in the area. He came to see them.'

'Why didn't you tell me sooner?' demanded Kitty, leaping off the swingseat. 'Where is he? I must see him.'

'Follow me,' said Lucy. 'He's in Pilchard Way. At number 22.'

'He's a legend,' said Kitty trotting along beside her. 'There were five Alsatians, two Dobermann Pinschers and a Rottweiler. He sent them all running home with their tails between their legs.'

'It must have been quite a sight,' agreed Lucy. 'I wish I'd been there.'

'What a cat!' said Kitty.

They leapt over a fence, dodged down an alley way, crossed several gardens and cut into Pilchard Way via a short cut across the playing fields.

'They say the battle lasted for two hours,' said Kitty. 'And when it was over Eddie just went home and had his tea as though nothing had happened.'

They half walked, half ran along Pilchard Way.

'There he is,' whispered Lucy. She nodded towards a small group of cats on the other side of the road.

'Let's get closer,' said Kitty.

The two kittens crossed the road.

Eddie was talking to two cats and three

young kittens. They were all looking at him adoringly. He looked over as Kitty and Lucy approached and raised a questioning eyebrow.

'I hope you don't mind,' said Kitty. 'We just wanted to see you.'

'You're a legend,' said Lucy.

Eddie laughed. 'Why am I a legend?' he asked.

'The Battle of Langham Drive,' said Kitty.

Eddie laughed again. 'You mustn't believe everything you hear,' he said. 'Things get exaggerated.'

'But you were attacked by eight huge dogs!' said Kitty.

'That's true,' agreed Eddie. 'Though three of them were poodles.'

'And they all went home with their tails between their legs,' said Lucy.

'While you went home unscathed!' added Kitty. 'You're our hero.'

'I didn't fight any dogs that day,' said Eddie.

Lucy and Kitty looked at him, confused. 'What do you mean?' asked Kitty.

'I went up a tree,' laughed Eddie. 'It was the sensible thing to do. I went up a tree and stayed there until they all went home. They'd have torn me limb from limb.'

'But the legend . . . ' said Kitty.

'I don't know where that came from,' said Eddie. He shrugged. 'Tales are told. Exaggerations made. A small drama becomes a huge victory.'

'Oh,' said Kitty. She felt disappointed.

'I'm sorry if you feel let down,' said Eddie. 'But I'm not going to lie to you. It wouldn't be right.'

'No,' said Lucy.

'It was nice to meet you anyway,' said Kitty.

'Yes. Very nice,' added Lucy.

The two kittens turned and headed back for home.

For a while neither of them spoke. 'It was very honest of him to tell us the truth,' said Kitty eventually.

'Yes,' agreed Lucy. 'But in a way I wish he

hadn't. I liked the story the way it was.'

'Me too,' admitted Kitty.

There was a silence again.

'He was probably just being modest,' said Lucy.

Kitty looked at her half sister. 'You're probably right,' she agreed.

'A hero like Eddie would be modest,' said Lucy.

'Isn't he amazing,' said Kitty. 'I think he's even more of a hero now,' she added after a moment. 'To be so brave and to win such a huge battle and then to pretend it didn't happen that way.'

'A real super hero,' agreed Lucy.

And so another page was added to Eddie's legend.

Moral

History is sometimes more a matter of romantic perception than of hard fact. And that's often because that's the way we prefer it.

Memories And Dreams

Beatrice had lived in the country for nine years when her Uprights decided to sell their country home, together with its wonderful garden, and purchase an apartment in the centre of the city.

Beatrice just couldn't understand it. She knew that most Uprights move from the city to the country; selling their highly priced city nest and using the proceeds to purchase a small estate in the countryside.

Her Uprights just had to be different.

Beatrice knew she was going to be miserable in the city.

She'd loved living in the country.

The house they'd shared had contained an almost endless supply of surprises and delights. Two staircases — one ornate and rather grand and one fiddly and winding. Huge fireplaces in which the Uprights had burnt great chunks of tree. Cupboards, nooks and crannies galore. A large cellar and a vast attic.

And the garden!

She had always loved the garden that she and the Uprights had shared.

Trees and shrubs providing shade on hot

summer days. Oaks, elms and a willow tree. A chestnut tree and a walnut tree. Huge trees like cathedrals. Beautiful flower beds, filled with plants of every imaginable colour (and some unimaginable delights) attracting an almost endless variety of butterflies. A rock garden full of alpine plants. A summerhouse. A large lawn. A pond. A stream at the bottom of the garden.

And, on the other side of the fence, endless fields of corn and wheat.

All this had now gone.

And in its place there was a small, noisy apartment in the centre of a large, dirty city.

She was woken early in the morning by the tooting and hooting of angry taxi drivers taking businessmen to their meetings. She was woken late at night by the tooting and hooting of angry taxi drivers taking revellers to and from their night clubs.

If the noises were unbearable the smells were even worse. The suffocating stench of diesel fumes and sweaty Uprights rushing hither and thither, all mixed with stale cooking smells from restaurants in the streets down below.

Beatrice didn't like it. She didn't like any of it.

She missed the trees, the nooks, the butterflies, the mice, the mooing cows, the

staircases, the crannies, the dew lad
the beetles and the noises and smel
countryside.

She missed them all very much in

She lay on the sofa (which was tne same
sofa she'd always lain on because the
Uprights had, thank heavens, brought it with
them) and dreamt of those, now far off, days
in the country.

She closed her eyes and dreamt of chasing
mice and dancing with butterflies. In her
dreams she always caught the mice she
chased. And every dance with a butterfly was
gloriously elegant. Never, in her dreams, did
she topple into a bed of pansies and have to
spring away to escape her embarrassment.

She dreamt of the joy of finding a new, cosy
hiding place where she could settle down for
a snooze on those oh-so-common weekends
when visitors interrupted her routine.

She dreamt of the days when, to avoid the
storms outside, she had curled up in front of
a raging log fire. (And she quickly erased
from her memory the times when a spark
from the fire had burnt her fur.)

She dreamt of moonbeams filtering through
attic windows and of spiders as big as mice.
(And she suppressed thoughts of cobwebs
that clung to her nose and made her sneeze.)

She dreamt of all the good things and she

ed all the unpleasant memories for that, after all, is the very best way to enjoy the past. She dreamt of things that would never be and savoured memories of things that had never been.

And there, lying on the sofa, her eyes firmly closed, she smiled in constant pleasure as she bathed in those glorious memories where everything was perfection, and every day was filled with unimpaired delights.

Moral

It doesn't matter where you live.
Where you live is really in your head.

The Worrier

Letitia worried about everything she could find to worry about. She worried about whether or not it was going to rain. She worried that it might be too hot, and dry up the lawn and the plants in the garden. She worried that if she said the wrong thing then other cats might think badly of her. And she worried that if she said the right thing other cats might think she was trying to be too good — and, therefore, think badly of her. She worried that if she decided to sit on the lap of one Upright, the other Upright might be upset. And she worried that if she sat on the lap of the Upright whose lap she hadn't decided to sit on then the Upright whose lap she had originally decided to sit on but later decided not to sit on might be hurt.

She worried about the butterflies. 'What will happen,' she asked her friend Emily, 'if they bump into one another? They never seem to be quite sure where they're going.'

She worried about the mice. 'They cause the Uprights a lot of worry,' she told Emily. 'The Upright who wears a Skirt is terrified of them.' But she worried that if she caught one she would cause unhappiness in the mouse's family. (Not to mention to the mouse itself.)

'You worry too much,' laughed Emily. 'You'll worry yourself ill. You should try and take life a little easier. Let the world wash over you. Don't take everything to heart.'

'I can't help it,' said Letitia, sadly. 'It's my nature.'

'Well, you must try not to worry,' said Emily. 'If you worry too much you'll make yourself ill.'

'I know,' said Letitia softly. 'But I really can't help myself.'

When Emily went missing and didn't turn up for tea the Uprights were quite unconcerned. They were confident that there was nothing seriously the matter.

'She'll turn up,' said the Upright in Trousers. 'She's probably stalking a mouse in the tool shed.'

'Or halfway up a tree watching a bird,' suggested the Upright who wears a Skirt.

They sat down to their fish fingers and baked beans and thought no more about it.

But Letitia worried.

She was so worried that she couldn't eat. (Even

though it was her favourite food for tea.) She went out into the garden to look for Emily.

She looked in the shed but Emily wasn't there.

She looked up every tree in the garden.

But Emily wasn't up a tree.

She looked in the road — terrified, suddenly, that Emily might have had an accident. Her heart beat twice as fast as usual as she searched the gutters and the grass verges.

But, to her great relief, Emily wasn't there.

Letitia went back into the house and looked in the airing cupboard. Just in case Emily had fallen asleep.

But she wasn't there.

Letitia looked in the garage.

Emily wasn't in the garage.

By now Letitia was more than concerned. She was definitely very worried.

She climbed over the fence and into a piece of rough ground at the bottom of their garden. She didn't like it there. She found it frightening.

But she loved Emily very much. She loved Emily more than she feared the waste land. She worried about Emily more than she worried about the rats and foxes and other beasties that might be hiding in the long grass. And so she searched for her friend.

Letitia had almost given up when she heard the very faintest of miaows.

'Miaow.'

It was hardly there.

But Letitia heard it. And she headed towards it.

'Emily?' she called. 'Are you there?'

'I'm over here.'

Letitia rushed towards the sound of her friend's voice.

'I'm stuck,' said Emily sadly. She had been crying. And her throat was raw with calling. She was caught in a hawthorn hedge. Someone had thrown a curl of barbed wire into the hedge and somehow Emily had got her rear legs caught in the wire.

'If I press down on the wire and you lift up your right rear leg you can get it free,' said Letitia.

Emily did as her friend suggested.

'Now the other leg.'

Emily freed the other leg.

Letitia lifted her paw off the barbed wire. A barb on the wire had cut into her and she was bleeding.

'Oh dear!' said Emily. 'You've cut yourself.'

'It doesn't matter,' said Letitia, who meant it. 'As long as you're safe.'

Side by side, the two cats headed back for home. And safety.

'I'm so glad you came for me,' whispered Emily.

'So am I,' answered Letitia.

'I was frightened no one would find me and I would be there all night in the dark,' said Emily.

'I couldn't have rested until I'd found you,' said Letitia.

'You're a good and true friend,' said Emily.

'And a worrier,' said Letitia.

'Yes,' agreed Emily. 'It's lucky for me that you are.'

Moral

**Not all worriers are good and kind.
But everything good and kind comes
from worriers.**

The Good Samaritan

Tarki was a sensitive, kind and thoughtful cat. He always tried to make sure that nothing he did ever upset anyone else. He hated to see other cats unhappy. Sometimes, however, he found that his altruistic way of life made things rather more difficult than they might otherwise have been.

One day, for example, he was sitting in his garden, sunning himself in mid-morning sunshine, when he heard a call from a neighbouring garden.

'What's up?' Tarki called. He really wanted to stay where he was — it was a long time since he'd managed to spend a morning doing nothing much — but the call had sounded urgent.

'I need some help!' came the reply. Tarki recognised the voice of a tabby cat called Simon who lived with an elderly Upright in a small house just a few gardens away.

Without hesitating, or stopping to ask why Simon needed help, Tarki got up and padded over to the fence which surrounded his Uprights' garden. He slipped easily between the posts, crossed the next garden, jumped over a solid wooden fence, crossed another garden and leapt over a third fence.

'Hello!' he said, brightly. 'What's the matter? How can I help you?'

Simon, who was lying beside a fish pond, looked up. 'I need help with this goldfish,' he answered. 'If you could make some splashing noises over the other side of the pond then the fish will swim towards me and I can catch it.'

Keen to be of help Tarki went round to the other side of the pond. Reluctantly, he dipped a paw into the water and splashed away. Tarki hated getting his fur wet and, to make matters worse, the water was cold.

'Got it!' cried Simon, a few moments later. He hauled a fish out of the pond. He looked very pleased with himself.

'Is that all you needed?' asked Tarki.

'That's all, thanks,' said Simon. He seemed very grateful. Tarki felt so pleased that he didn't notice that Simon was too busy concentrating on his catch to have the decency to offer to share the fish.

Tarki headed back for home. He wasn't always thanked for his kindnesses and courtesies and it always made him feel good when he was.

'Oi!' called another cat as Tarki began his journey homewards.

Tarki turned.

'Oi!' repeated the cat. It was a large black and white cat with a piece bitten out of one ear. 'What do you think you're doing?'

'I've just been helping Simon,' explained Tarki. 'He needed some assistance with a goldfish.'

'You crossed my garden,' complained the cat. He sounded very bad-tempered.

'It was the only way to get there,' explained Tarki. 'I didn't do any hunting while I was in your garden. I just passed through. I was helping another cat.'

'Next time you want to cross my territory you make sure that you ask!' snapped the cat.

'Sorry,' apologised Tarki. He now felt rather sad. He couldn't understand why cats were sometimes so quick to moan; so quick to find fault where none had been intended. He went home, lay down and went back to sleep. Doing good turns was, he decided, getting more difficult by the day.

An hour or so later he was woken by another call. This time it came from the bottom of the garden.

'What's the matter?' Tarki called.

'I'm stuck!' cried a strange voice.

Tarki looked around. He couldn't see where the voice was coming from.

'I'm up here!' said the voice. 'Up a tree!'

Tarki looked up. And sure enough there

was a kitten up a tree on the other side of the fence at the bottom of his garden. The kitten wasn't very high — perhaps a third of the way up — but it looked terrified.

'How did you get up there?' asked Tarki.

'I climbed up,' answered the kitten.

'Can't you get down?' Tarki asked.

'I'm too frightened,' replied the kitten.

'Wait there,' said Tarki. 'I'll get you down in a jiffy.'

And he did.

'I've done two good deeds today,' he said to himself as he lay back down on the grass. 'And got into trouble twice.'

By coaxing and cajoling and pulling and holding he managed to help the kitten down the trunk and onto the grass. The kitten, still shivering with fear, was very grateful.

'Hey you!' cried an angry sounding Upright.

Tarki looked up.

A fierce looking Upright was marching across a neatly trimmed lawn towards them.

'What have you been doing up that tree?' demanded the Upright.

'I was just . . . ,' began Tarki.

'You'd better run,' murmured the kitten. 'My Upright can be very fierce. He doesn't like other cats coming into our garden and climbing our trees.'

And so, without waiting to discuss or to explain, Tarki left. He leapt back over the fence and went back into his own garden.

'I've done two good deeds today,' he said to himself as he lay back down on the grass. 'And got into trouble twice.' He sighed.

'What a strange, strange world it is,' Tarki thought to himself. 'One good turn may deserve another. But we don't always get what we deserve.'

Moral

If you limit your actions to the things no one can find fault with, you will not do very much.

The Rebel

'We're going to the park!' said Hetty, a five-year-old Persian. 'Do you want to come with us?'

'I can't,' said Ollie, a two-year-old white, short-haired cat. 'My Uprights have said I'm not to go to the park.'

'But you won't be by yourself,' said Hetty. 'There are four of us going. Five if you come.'

'No, I really can't,' said Ollie. 'I'll get into terrible trouble if I do.'

'But they won't find out,' said Hetty. 'We'll be back before teatime. They'll just think you've been asleep somewhere.'

'No, I mustn't,' said Ollie, rather sadly. He really wanted to go to the park. And he knew he'd be safe enough with Hetty and the others. But he'd been told not to. And he didn't like being disobedient. So, he lay back down, closed his eyes and tried to pretend he was happier staying where he was.

He hadn't been asleep for more than ten minutes when he was woken again. This time it was by James, a three-year-old mackerel tabby.

'The Mackintoshes, the Uprights at number 12, put a chicken carcass in their dustbin last night,' said James. 'Percy says that if there are three of us we can take the lid off their bin and get it out.'

'I'm not allowed to eat food out of dustbins,' said Ollie.

'Why on earth not?' asked James, genuinely puzzled.

'I'm not allowed to eat food out of dustbins," said Ollie.

'I don't know,' replied Ollie, who didn't.

'Well that's a silly rule,' said James.

'I know it is,' agreed Ollie.

'So are you coming?'

'No. I mustn't. I've been told not to.'

'Well, that's a shame,' said James. And he rushed off to try and find someone else to help them get the lid off the Mackintosh's dustbin.

Ollie lay down and tried to go back to sleep.

But he felt rather sad.

He wasn't a natural rebel but it did sometimes seem to him that perhaps his Uprights might be rather too keen on making rules.

Going to the park would have been fun. And he would have really enjoyed helping James and Percy drag the chicken carcass out of the Mackintoshs' dustbin. What harm could it have possibly done?

He thought about it. And thought about it again.

'Wait!' he called to James.

James turned.

'I'm coming!' Ollie shouted. 'Let's go and get that chicken!' James grinned and waited for him.

Moral

Sometimes, a cat has just got to do what a cat's got to do. And when there is a chicken carcass in the dustbin the rules have to go out of the window.

Looking Down At Birds

'Come and look!' called Gerry.

Robbie, who was peering inside a flower, trying to see where the bumble bee had gone, went over to see what Gerry wanted him to look at.

'Up the tree!' said Gerry, who always spoke as though each sentence ended in an exclamation mark.

Robbie looked up. 'I can't see anything,' he said.

136

'Higher!' said Gerry. 'You have to look higher!'

Robbie looked higher. And when he saw what Gerry was talking about he could hardly believe his eyes. 'Golly,' he said. 'Gosh.'

'It's Bubbles!' said Gerry.

'I know it is,' said Robbie.

'He's right at the very top of the tree!'

'Yes,' agreed Robbie, who could see that.

They stood for a while and stared at their older neighbour as he walked out on a narrow branch and sat down. The branch was so narrow that it bent down under his weight. The two kittens held their breath.

'How long has he been up there?' asked Robbie.

'I don't know,' said Gerry. 'I only saw him a few moments ago. I was watching a bird fly up into the tree.'

'What's he going to do now?' asked Robbie.

'I don't know!' said Gerry.

The two of them stood and watched. And eventually Bubbles walked back along the branch and climbed down the tree trunk. He came down very quickly, either because that was the way he normally descended trees or because gravity had overcome natural prudence.

'That was something else!' said Gerry.

'It was,' agreed Robbie, who, like Gerry, wasn't quite sure what the phrase meant but thought it sounded very grown up.

They waited until Bubbles had returned to ground level and then turned away. Gerry went back to whatever he was doing before and Robbie, who had forgotten what he had been doing before, chased a butterfly around some tulips.

But the sight of Bubbles walking around high up in the tree stayed with him. It was the first time he'd seen a cat up a tree. And he knew it was something he wanted to try for himself.

'Have you ever thought of climbing a tree yourself?' Robbie asked Gerry a few minutes later.

Gerry stared at him and swallowed. 'Climb a tree?' he said. 'Right up a tree?'

'Well not necessarily right up a tree,' admitted Robbie. 'But perhaps climb up a bit of a tree.'

'I don't know,' said Gerry. He wasn't exactly frightened. Cautious, perhaps. 'When I'm older maybe!'

'I want to do it now,' said Robbie.

And, without another word, he raced off to the base of the tree that Bubbles had climbed so successfully just a little earlier in the day.

When he got to the bottom of the trunk he

looked up. The tree seemed to go up and up and up. It reached right up to the sky. 'If I go right to the top, will I be able to climb onto a cloud?' Robbie wondered to himself. He had always thought clouds might be fun to play with.

He walked back a pace or two and then took a run at the tree.

It took him four tries to reach the lowest branch, which was only about six feet off the ground. He looked down at Gerry. To a kitten, six feet up a tree is a long way.

'You look quite small from up here!' he said.

'I am quite small!' said Gerry.

'No. You look smaller than usual,' said Robbie.

'So do you!' agreed Gerry.

Robbie looked around. If he climbed up another few feet of tree he would, he thought, be able to climb out onto a branch which reached right out above Gerry's head.

He climbed up a little more and reached the branch he was aiming at. Carefully, slowly, tentatively, he walked out along it.

The feeling was like nothing he'd ever felt before. This was far, far more exciting than watching another cat climb a tree.

He sat down on the branch for a moment and looked around. There were branches below him now. He watched a butterfly dance around underneath him. And then a bird flew by underneath him.

A BIRD FLEW BY UNDERNEATH HIM!

'Are you going higher?' shouted Gerry, though in fact Robbie wasn't so high that he needed to shout.

'Not this time,' replied Robbie. He decided that he'd gone far enough. He wanted to go down. Suddenly, he very much wanted to go down. He made his way back along the branch to the trunk of the tree and then slithered and slid and half fell back to the ground.

'That wasn't very elegant!' said Gerry accurately but rather unkindly.

'I don't care!' said Robbie, who genuinely didn't. He was excited and exhilarated by his climb.

'You didn't go as high as Bubbles!' said Gerry.

'I know,' said Robbie. 'But it was far more exciting to go up that bit of the tree than it was to watch Bubbles go right to the top!'

'Was it really?' asked Gerry doubtfully. He didn't sound at all convinced.

'Definitely!' said Robbie. 'You just wait and see if you don't believe me.'

And when Gerry eventually plucked up the

courage to climb up the tree for the first time he discovered, much to his surprise, that Robbie was absolutely right. Climbing a quarter of the way up a tree by yourself is far more thrilling than watching another cat climb all the way up the tree.

Moral

A modest first hand experience always beats a spectacular second hand experience.

Badgers and Foxes And Dangerous Beasties

'Let's go for a walk in the woods,' said Kerry.

'I'm frightened of the woods,' said Tipper. 'There are badgers and foxes and all sorts of dangerous beasties there.'

'Don't be silly,' said Kerry. 'That's a myth. There are no foxes or badgers living in the woods. We won't find anything larger than a field mouse there. And there are plenty of those.'

Tipper wasn't so sure. He'd heard some terrible stories about cats who had wandered into the woods and been chased out by foxes. And, from a friend of a friend of a friend, he'd heard about a cat who'd been very nearly eaten alive by a badger.

'We can have great fun in the woods!' insisted Kerry. 'There are heaps of trees to climb. And there are rotten tree stumps teeming with creatures. We can run through the bushes and hide in the undergrowth. There are thousands of wonderful smells and sights in the woods.'

Tipper still wasn't happy about it, but,

'We can have good fun in the woods!' insisted
Kerry. 'There are heaps of trees to climb.'

because Kerry was his friend, and because Kerry was so certain, he agreed to go with him.

At first everything went wonderfully well.

The two friends climbed two trees, chased several mice and stared in amazement at the huge township living in a hollowed out fallen oak.

Then things went wrong.

It was Tipper who was the first to see the fox.

'Psst!' he said. 'Look over there!'

'What is it?' asked Kerry.

'I know you said there aren't any foxes in the wood,' said Tipper. 'But it *looks* like a fox.'

Kerry looked.

It was a fox.

'It is a fox,' said Kerry in a whisper. 'Whoops.'

'What do we do now?' asked Tipper.

'Do you think it's seen us?'

'It's looking our way. And it's sniffing the air.'

'It's seen us,' said Kerry.

'So, what do we do?'

'We run,' said Kerry. 'We run very quickly. And we run now.'

He and Tipper turned and raced as fast as they could towards the edge of the woods.

They just managed to stay ahead of the fox.

Half an hour later, still breathless, and recovering from their brush with the fox, Tipper and Kerry lay on the lawn.

'I'm sorry,' said Kerry. 'I was wrong about there not being any foxes in the wood.'

'You were,' agreed Tipper.

'It was a mistake,' said Kerry.

'It was,' agreed Tipper.

'I don't think we should go there again,' said Kerry. Tipper looked at him. 'I think that's a very wise suggestion,' he said.

'Well, I always try to learn from my mistakes,' said Kerry.

'So do I,' said Tipper.

Kerry looked at him.

'I've learned not to take too much notice of you when you say you're sure about something,' said Tipper with a smile.

Moral

***Apologising for your mistakes is a
sign of strength.
Learning from your mistakes is a
sign of maturity.***

The Big Bully

Frank was the biggest cat anyone in the neighbourhood had ever seen.

Most big cats are very gentle and peaceful creatures. They do a lot of sleeping and eating and purring but they don't throw their weight around.

But Frank wasn't gentle and he wasn't peaceful.

He was a terrible bully.

Everyone was scared of him.

Frank knew this and took full advantage of it. He forced all the other cats to treat him like some sort of Emperor. If they caught a mouse he reserved the right to demand that they give it to him. If they found a particularly pleasant sleeping spot and he wanted it then he would simply take it. If he wanted them to do something for him then he would tell them to do it — and expect instant obedience. If a cat dared to stand up to him he would snarl and hiss and since he was very large and very good at snarling and hissing this usually had the desired effect.

Naturally, the cats and the kittens in the neighbourhood didn't like Frank very much. In fact, they really didn't like him at all.

Most of them accepted his malevolent ways with the same sort of resignation that they accepted rain and dogs.

'Things like rain, dogs and Frank are a part of life and there isn't much you can do about them,' said Jules.

But Philip found it difficult to be so philosophical about the local bully.

'I hate him,' he told everyone who would listen. 'I hate him, I hate him, I hate him.'

And hate him he did.

Day and night he dreamt of being able to find a way to punish Frank for his bullying ways.

He gave up all his other interests to concentrate on hating Frank.

He gave up climbing trees, teasing the neighbour's dog and sleeping in the airing cupboard.

All his energy went into hating the bully.

Frank knew about it, of course.

But he didn't care.

He wasn't frightened of Philip. He knew that if it came to a fight then he would win. Easily. Force is the only thing bullies understand and respect.

In the end Philip's anger made him quite ill. He lost his appetite and his fur started to fall out.

'Your anger is eating you up,' his friends told him. 'You must stop hating Frank and start enjoying your life again.'

'But it's so unfair that he should get away with it,' said Philip.

'You're right,' they told him. 'It is unfair. But that isn't going to change things. And meanwhile you've lost your appetite and your fur is falling out while Frank is still the local bully.'

But Philip couldn't change his ways.

His hatred burnt up inside him. He developed ulcers and heart trouble. And eventually he died.

Meanwhile, Frank was still the local bully.

Moral

Hate invariably does more damage to the person doing the hating than to the object of their hatred.

Sunshine And Butterflies

It had been raining for days. Steady, boring rain. The sort that you hardly notice at first. The sort that doesn't really seem to be rain until you've been out in it for ten minutes. The sort that soaks you before you realise that you're even getting wet.

It was windy too. One of those swirling, cold annoying winds that grabs up all the old leaves and bits of garden rubbish and throws them about.

Ricky and Sam were indoors, lying on the window seat and feeling rather sorry for themselves.

They weren't having a good time.

Their Upright had forgotten to go to the big shop and so had had to purchase their tinned food from the corner shop in the village. And the corner shop in the village only sold the really cheap food that tasted as though the people selling it hated cats.

The Upright had had unexpected visitors too. And the unexpected visitors had drunk all the available milk in their tea.

So the only liquid in the cats' bowls was water. Water straight from the tap. It stank of

'Wake up,' he whispered
'Why?' demanded Sam grumpily.
'Because the sun is coming out,' said Ricky
'And I just saw two butterflies.'

chlorine and tasted like poison.

The builders were busy upstairs. They had taken over the spare bedroom, the bathroom and the airing cupboard. Three of the cats' favourite sleeping spots were now out of bounds. And the whole house shook with the sound of hammering and the raucous, empty chatter of radio disc jockeys.

'The only thing I hate more than cheap cat food is the noise of the radio,' said Ricky.

'I'm not sure about that,' said Sam. He thought for a while. 'No,' he said at last. 'I hate cheap cat food more than I hate the noise of the radio.'

'Both are horrid,' said Ricky.

'Both are horrid,' agreed Sam.

'Generally speaking, I think it's fair to say that it's not been a good week,' said Ricky.

'One darned thing after another,' said Sam.

'I think I'll have a snooze,' said Ricky.

'Good idea,' agreed Sam.

'Maybe things will be better when we wake up,' said Ricky.

'I don't think they can be any worse,' said Sam.

Ricky was the first to wake. He sat up and looked out of the window. The rain had stopped, the wind had died down and the builders were climbing into their van, ready to set off to the pub for their lunch.

He tapped Sam on the shoulder. 'Wake up,' he whispered.

'Why?' demanded Sam, grumpily.

'Because the sun is coming out,' said Ricky. 'And I just saw two butterflies.'

Moral

Life sometimes seems to be just one darned thing after another. And then the sun comes out and a butterfly flutters into view and suddenly things seem a whole lot better.

We do hope that you have enjoyed reading this large print book.

Did you know that all of our titles are available for purchase?

We publish a wide range of high quality large print books including:
Romances, Mysteries, Classics
General Fiction
Non Fiction and Westerns

Special interest titles available in large print are:
The Little Oxford Dictionary
Music Book
Song Book
Hymn Book
Service Book

Also available from us courtesy of Oxford University Press:
Young Readers' Dictionary
(large print edition)
Young Readers' Thesaurus
(large print edition)

For further information or a free brochure, please contact us at:
Ulverscroft Large Print Books Ltd.,
The Green, Bradgate Road, Anstey,
Leicester, LE7 7FU, England.
Tel: (00 44) 0116 236 4325
Fax: (00 44) 0116 234 0205